Fated to the Enemy Alpha

A SHIFTER PARANORMAL ROMANCE

Ruby Brinks

Copyrights

Copyright © 2023 by Ruby Brinks

All rights reserved.

No part of this publication may be reproduced, distributed, or transmitted in any form or by any means, including photocopying, recording, or other electronic or mechanical methods, without the prior written permission of the publisher, except as permitted by U.S. copyright law.

The story, all names, characters, and incidents portrayed in this production are fictitious. No identification with actual persons (living or deceased), places, buildings, and products is intended or should be inferred.

1st edition July 2023

Contents

1. Prologue — 1
2. Chapter 1 — 4
3. Chapter 2 — 8
4. Chapter 3 — 15
5. Chapter 4 — 25
6. Chapter 5 — 34
7. Chapter 6 — 38
8. Chapter 7 — 44
9. Chapter 8 — 51
10. Chapter 9 — 62
11. Chapter 10 — 68
12. Chapter 11 — 75
13. Chapter 12 — 83
14. Chapter 13 — 89
15. Chapter 14 — 95

16.	Chapter 15	103
17.	Chapter 16	118
18.	Chapter 17	127
19.	Chapter 18	135
20.	Chapter 19	140
21.	Chapter 20	147
22.	Chapter 21	155
23.	Chapter 22	163
24.	Chapter 23	166
25.	Chapter 24	174
26.	Epilogue	183
27.	Get a Steamy Alpha Romance for FREE!	190

Prologue

"Here comes the sun, doo-doo-doo-doo,

   Here comes the sun, and I say,

   It's alright..."

My voice isn't melodious, yet it seems to comfort the hazel wolf lying in my arms. He bleeds, staining the ground crimson, and his whimper is slow and agony-filled. I want to run away, to get him some help, but when I try to move, he whimpers once more, louder. His body shifts closer on top of mine, and his hind leg covers my own.

His fur has lost its sheen, and his breathing is so shallow. Tears cascade down my face like waterfalls. The tears zig zag under my chin, and I feel hopeless as I comb his fur with my fingers.

I place my forehead to his nose, allowing him to sniff me. He already asked me not to save him, but he's important to me... special. I release my grip on his fur and outstretch my hands, connecting to the water supply from a nearby creek. The water comes to me when I call it, like a close friend. It freely moves over my feet, but my shoes do not get wet. The water washes over my body, and as an extension, covers the wolf. He takes a deep breath, an inhale of life as the water blankets him. His deep and bloody scratches are now healing. His skin is knitting back together.

"I'm sorry," I whisper and place a kiss on his cheek and continue stroking his fur....His body begins to shake violently, as though he's convulsing, and his eyes strike the back of his lids...

Until I'm awake in my office, jolted from something that feels like a memory by a ringing phone. I reach for my water bottle sitting at the edge of my desk and take a swig before picking it up. My throat has gone dry due to another confusing yet familiar dream.

It's been the same dream every night for the last month. I can't shake it, and I relive it constantly.

Before the shrilling ring of my phone stops, I pick it up with hope in my heart. I'm expecting a phone call, and I'm hoping that it's the one I've been waiting for.

"Thank you for calling Sanderson's Realty Group. This is Mira speaking..."

I wait to hear Jaxon's voice, hoping that he's ready to sell the Loch Bar & Grill, and I can finally put the issue of acquiring his business to rest. Yet, it is not his voice on the other end I hear.

"I'm on my way into your office," Mr. Sanderson says and hangs up in my face. He must have called me from his car or cell, because the caller ID didn't pick up his desk phone. If he's coming into my office, that can't be good.

I slap the phone down on its receiver in irritation and scan my office for anything that might be out of place. The last thing I need is for my compulsive boss to come into my office telling me what else I'm doing wrong. Outside the obvious fact of getting Jaxon Coolidge to sell us his bar.

Chapter 1

Mira

"I'll cut right to it. Where are we with the Loch Bar & Grill?" Mr. Sanderson questions me as though I'm just another flunkie who works for him. I've given years to this company, and at times, I still feel like a peon just waiting for my chance. Normally, my success rate is high and can't be refuted. But, Jaxon Coolidge is the bane of my existence.

"I've had no luck. I've left several messages for Mr. Coolidge, and I am not getting anywhere. When he does respond, he waits until it's overnight, and his voicemails are... directive, but harsh," I admit and, lean back in my seat. I huff out a sigh of frustration and place my head against the headrest of my desk chair.

"I see. Play me the voicemails," Mr. Sanderson directs and takes a seat across from me. He crosses his left leg over his right and leans in, as though he's expecting to hear something that I haven't already said.

I play the first voicemail, which is nothing more but an introduction. From the thickness of his voice, I can tell he's stern, and perhaps a large man.

The next voicemail plays automatically, and the next. Mr. Sanderson seems to be waiting for something to catch his attention, but Jaxon is only saying what I've told Mr. Sanderson time and time again. He isn't interested in selling, and he's put his foot down about it.

It isn't until the last message that Mr. Sanderson seems to have found the light switch in his brain.

"Listen, if the Sanderson Realty Group wants to purchase Loch, you could at least have the common decency to come down here and ask for it in my face. Where I'm from, that's how we do things..."

He has an accent that doesn't mimic that of city life. If he weren't being such a pain in my ass, I'd say his voice was even sexy.

"It sounds clear to me what Mr. Coolidge wants, Mira. If a trip to the mountains is what it will take—"

"The mountains? Oh, Mr. Sanderson, I don't know about that. I'm not really the outdoorsy type. My shoes... not to mention I've never really been in the field. I'd probably be much better right here. You could send—"

"You will be just fine. Don't forget, your promotion is on the line if this deal falls through. I'd hate to see you miss out on an amazing opportunity because you're afraid to get your hands dirty, quite literally."

Mr. Sanderson stands from his seat and heads toward the door. He doesn't give me another opportunity to say anything as he edges toward the knob. Before twisting it, he looks over his shoulder and says, "This place could use some dusting. Have Christina come in and redo it," and then leaves my office with his round about ultimatum.

If I don't take this project on personally, I won't get my promotion, and I deserve it. I'm not like the others here with privilege—their way was paid into this office. I, on the other hand, had to fight, crawl, and work my ass off to get here. I'm a city girl through and through but there's no way I'd let a little dirt stand in my way.

This promotion would grant me the opportunity to live a lifestyle that I only dreamed about growing up.

I wasn't doing too bad now, but more money meant I could continue to feed my shoe addiction and start looking into designing my own dream home.

Working with a group of realtors had shown me a lot, and in my late twenties, I'm so glad I didn't purchase a home. There were aspects of the home buying process that I wouldn't have learned without becoming a licensed realtor. My dream home was a major item still on my bucket list.

Getting that promotion would change my life, and ultimately, change my circumstances.

I'll just have to go see Mr. Coolidge in person, and hopefully, he'll make it worth my while....

Chapter 2

JAXON

Papers go flying off my large and stacked desk. I can't see myself out of the mess my father has created for me, literally. I've been organizing and reorganizing for weeks trying to make this office somewhat operable, but to no avail.

My fingers instinctively scratch through the unusual fullness of my dirty blonde beard. It's been weeks since I've had time to shave, let alone get a haircut. Its shagginess hovering over the nape of my neck is a sad reminder.

Why my father would leave me Loch Bar & Grill behooves me. Each moment I spend in this dying bar is another moment I'm neglecting my *family*. My father's death shoved me into becoming the alpha. I always knew it would happen someday, but I didn't expect that day to be any time soon. My father was a warrior, a god amongst men, and his loss has impacted the pack deeper than even I could have ever imagined. A sickness, cancer, like a thief in the night, came and stole his life right from underneath him. Within two months of his diagnosis, he was taken.

His dying wish was that I oversee the Bar & Grill, and I've been doing the best I can, but I'd much rather be tending to the pack. I have two major responsibilities now, and I'm not sure how to multi-task doing them both, not to mention the sale my dad left on the table with Sanderson Realty Group. He'd apparently been entertaining the thought of selling the bar. I wish he would have because then his financial troubles wouldn't be on my mind.

However, it was his last wish that I take care of things, so I can't believe that he'd want to actually get rid of the place. I'm doing the best I can to manage this place, but it hasn't exactly been easy. Between catching up on the bills and mortgage, I completely blew my own personal savings, and I refuse to take out a loan, simply because I need time to rebuild my finances.

But I'm making pennies when I do payroll, and the bartender and cook are literally being paid from my personal account. Knocking the papers off of the desk has done nothing but make the room an even bigger mess than it already was. I don't know how the old wolf made any sense of all this paperwork that's stacked a mile high in every corner of his office.

On the ground, I begin shuffling the papers to put them in some type of order when I hear the front door open. The footsteps are familiar, along with the scent. There is a knock at my door, and I invite the visitor in.

"Jax, what the hell is going on in here?" Pike, my beta asks. His brows are deeply furrowed as his green eyes scan the room.

"I'm… organizing," I respond while getting to my feet to greet him. I clap him on the shoulder and pick up the first stack of papers I've managed to put back together and place them on the desk.

"Yeah, okay. Well, I've come because I need to speak to you about something important."

"More important than the mountains of paperwork in this room? I can't wait." My tone is sarcastic, but the meaning of the sentiment is the same.

"Much more important. I've been trying to tell you for weeks, and maybe now you'll listen to me. There's something in the forest lurking. There are too many knicks in the trees. There's a feeling of unrest near the water—"

"You know that the water cannot be controlled, it can only be manipulated for a time," I interject. As my beta, I respect his opinion and his observation. But, I'd need more to go on than just a feeling.

"Yes, we wield power to temporarily manipulate the water, but something is still off. I tried to speak with the record keeper about it, but she won't leave her cabin and ignores me," he says, and a chuckle leaves my slightly parted lips. I'm not surprised to hear this. The record keeper doesn't think she owes anyone, most of all not a beta, any answers. She'd give them to me, but I can't be certain there's a real problem growing in the forest. There's always something out there, but between managing this place and being the alpha, I'm torn between responsibilities and haven't had an opportunity to assess the situation myself.

"Of course not. She's the record keeper and doing her job. It could be an omega, or maybe another shifter, but

I seriously doubt it's anything serious. Pike, bring me evidence that there's something going on, and I promise I'll take your concerns seriously," I finish and go back to separating the large stacks of paperwork.

Pike huffs with defeat, though he doesn't understand I'm trying to do what's best for everyone. If I start investigating a "threat" in the forest, the pack will worry. I can't afford another big shift like this. They've been gracious in giving me time to handle Dad's affairs, but the pack needs a leader who can lead, juggle, be strong, and somehow manage their human lives as well. The instability that comes with worry is already overwhelming enough. For now, I must focus on getting the human side of things in order, and then, if the need arises for help in the forest, I'll be the first person to take action.

"Alright then, I'll let you get back then... to your... work."

Pike slowly walks away, but I feel his eyes lingering on me as he leaves the room. I don't blame him—he's just as confused as I am. Pike is the only other person who knows about the possibility of selling the business.

On the one hand, the pack spends a lot of time here. It's been like a home to a lot of the community. It would be devastating if this place closed. On the other hand, Dad hardly charged people to be here, and that's why the place is struggling so bad now. Between the familiar locals not paying and creating the boundary between customer and pack member, it's been difficult to pull the business back together.

Not to mention that little city minx Mira Jefferson. She's persistent; I'll give her that. I'm sure with her fancy corner office in downtown Nashville and cushy life, she can't even begin to understand what kind of staple Loch Bar & Grill is to the mountain folk of the Appalachians. It brings a lot of us together and has kept us together since Dad was just a pup. His uncle passed the bar down to him, and then Dad onto me.

I take a seat at the desk, hoping I'll be able to find money to pay the staff for another two weeks. Sitting in my father's chair is heavy, like a bolder weighing on my conscience because my dad didn't have the courage to do something he should have. And now, I'm saddled with the same task. Sell or continue to worry in this business.

I'm a mechanic. I'm an alpha. That was the plan. Open my own garage, a shop of my own. That's how I've always made money, but I haven't been able to afford the time to stop and do anything that didn't involve this damn bar.

Before I can get lost too deeply in my thoughts, my phone alarm buzzes, indicating there's only 30 minutes until the lunch rush begins. It seems this is the only time the bar is busy with paying customers.

I'll have to put payroll on hold to go make some money. I'm racing against time, but our community cannot handle another big change. I'll just have to fight harder to keep Loch open.

Chapter 3

MIRA

"Are you sure this is where I'm supposed to get out?"

My vision is blurred by the profuse amount of rain blowing into view. It's muddy, smells like the great outdoors, and I didn't come dressed properly to be rained on.

"This is it. Welcome to the Appalachians," the driver, who introduced himself as 'Jo, with no e' at the airport says, a smile a mile long on his face. I nod my head and try to scale when I should open my door to step out. I checked the weather before I packed, and there was no rain in the forecast, yet, here it is, raining like a tsunami.

"Okay, thanks Jo. Let me just get my—"

"Oh, I wouldn't dream of letting a lady carry her own bags. Hold on, I'll grab 'em out the trunk…"

Jo, with no worries or cares at all, threw his small taxi-cab into park and slowly walked around to the trunk of his car as though it were sunshine and rainbows outside. Maybe he's used to the way the weather works here. Even when it rains in Nashville, it's not so murky that you can't see through it.

"Thanks, Jo." I hope he heard me before closing the door.

Jo grabs my bags and carries them to the front door of the boarding house I'm renting a room from. I was told there were no hotels within 50 miles of Loch Bar & Grill, which made Mama Susan's House the next best thing.

This town is like none I've seen. There are people freely moving about, and even holding full conversations through the wet chill. Though they are under awnings, the rain is freezing cold. Jo returns to the taxi and looks at me through the rearview mirror. I'm wondering if he can sense my uneasiness.

"Th-thank you, Jo," I say. I open the door to step out, not wanting him to have to wait around any longer than completely necessary.

"It's no problem. See ya around!" He calls over his shoulder, and he even waits until I take two full steps toward the door before pulling off. I'm almost at the door when my Doc Marten boots get stuck in the mud. Thank God the only thing I'm carrying is my purse or I would have been mortified or even would have completely fallen if I had anything else in my possession. The mud, though wet, seems to be hardening around me, and I only manage to get one boot out of the mud. I'm stuck, and I feel like I'm sinking. These boots are going to be completely ruined.

Those who are outside are laughing at me. I hear their whispers and snickers. I'm trying my hardest to shift my weight side to side to pull myself out of the mud, but nothing works. I want to scream, and I'm just about to when a man who looks like he's never seen a shower or washer and dryer comes over.

"Here, let me help you, Ms." His tone is polite enough, though his breath is offensive.

He wraps his robust arms around me and pulls me off my feet. A small yelp escapes my lips, and then he carries me to the concrete front of Ms. Susan's.

"Thank you very much," I say breathlessly, as though I'm the one who carried myself out of the mud.

"It's no problem, ma'am. I'm sure Mama Sue'll make sure you're good and warm. Go on in." The man nods his head toward the door, and I kindly nod back, pushing the door open. I drag my bags inside; they're as wet and filthy as I am now.

When I step over the threshold, I'm pleasantly surprised at the décor of the boarding house. It's contemporary and refreshing. The white and tan walls feel warm, bright, and welcoming. There are several photos on the wall, smiling faces. Nothing like what I expected from the outside of the almost log-looking cabin.

At the counter, there's a bell, several maps, and a plaque on the far-right side that reads "Best Boarding House 2018." That's somewhat comforting. I edge closer to the counter and almost jump out of my already very pale skin when an older woman rises to her full height. I didn't know she was standing there.

I gasp, shock rushing through me when she pops up.

"Good afternoon, you must be Mira Jefferson?" she questions, yet she says it with full confidence.

"Yes, ma'am, I am. How did you know?" My head tilts with curiosity.

"Simple. Everybody knows everybody around here, and from the way you're dressed, I know you don't live around here. But that's okay! I'm Susan, but you can call me Mama Sue."

Her smile is as bright as the lighting in this room, and it's... warming. Very friendly. Her rich tan skin shows little wrinkles, though there are age lines under her eyes.

Her gray hair hangs just above her shoulders which helps give away her age, though, I can tell from the way she's dressed, in a flannel and jeans, she's not your regular old woman.

"Well, Mama Sue, I'm Mira, it's nice to meet you," I return a greeting of my own, and she smiles a little more.

"Same to ya. If you don't mind me asking, what're you doin' in such a small town? You seem... big city. You got kin down here?" she asks, and I don't mind her inquisition since she's been so polite. I think of how to say I'm here on business politely, but it doesn't seem there is a way. Before I can form the words to speak, she interrupts me.

"You're lookin' to get something, aren't you?"

I smirk and nod my head since *I am* looking to get something. "Yes, ma'am, I am. I'm hopeful, anyway."

"I see. Well, our town might be small, but it has lots of wonders. I have no doubt you'll find something you weren't even looking for, along with whatever it is you've come to get. Let me get you checked in."

Her statement is ominous, but it piques my curiosity. I'm not sure what a town of less than 1,000 people have to offer me, nor am I sure of the "wonders" it could possess, but I'm open to finding out more.

Mama Sue turns toward the back wall, where there are rows of keys perfectly placed underneath their carved number. The key is the size of a door stop; very old school, but I like the old school meets contemporary look.

"Your room is on the second floor. Here is a menu for you to get some food if you're hungry. If you need anything, just pick up the phone in your room and dial one. Welcome to Mama Susan's, but you can call me—"

"Mama Sue. Thanks again," I grin and grab my bags and head toward the stairs. There are only ten or so steps that separate the first and second floor, something I'm thankful for. I can't imagine carrying these bags and my dirty body up another flight. Though there is another flight ahead of the second floor.

My room is the first off of the stairway, and when I twist the key in the knob and push, I'm met with a piney scent, along with a hint of mint. It's refreshing and clean.

I place my bags, key, and menu by the door and head over to the wooden desk and chair in the corner to remove my shoes to clean them. These won't hold dirt well. As I'm slipping off my shoes, a small black frame on the wall catches my eye.

"Home is where the orphaned feel safe."

The quote tugs on my heart. I suppose we're all orphans at some point. I stroll into the bathroom to rinse off my boots, and there are several sets of fresh towels and wash cloths, an extra blanket, and bars of soap tidily placed on a rack in the bathroom. There are toiletries, and the shower is beautiful. It resembles a cherry-stained oak with glass doors, and a tall shower head. Mama Sue has impeccable taste for such a small town, but I can tell she takes care of her visitors. It might not be so bad not staying in a hotel.

I leave my boots in the bathroom to dry off and head back into the main cabin. Easing down onto the bed, the mattress feels just the right amount of soft and firm, and it reminds me of my bed at home. I can tell I'll be comfortable here, until my stomach starts to growl. I wrap my arms around my waist, tugging at my shirt, as if someone other than myself can hear my stomach rumbling.

It's a good time to look at the menu. I lean over the bed and reach for the laminated menu and scan it. At the very top, the words "Loch Bar & Grill" are printed in bold, and this seems like fate. There's a picture of the entrance, settled by the marina. A dock entrance gives it a water feel. I knew I smelled something other than rain. Must be the fish in the river. My task is already at hand. At the bottom of the menu, are directions on how to order along with the mileage and directions to the place. It's raining cats and dogs outside, but if it's close enough, I can make my way over. It's less than 100 feet away. I must have not been paying attention to see it because of the rain.

Instead of attempting to place my boots on again, I choose a pair of my old Nikes. I like to do yoga in the morning, and I don't like slipping and sliding in my socks, so I brought my shoes along. Hopefully, they will fair better than my boots.

My shoes have been retrieved from my suitcase and I slip into them. I've memorized my order, not that it's a hard one; jumbo fried shrimp and French fries. I lock up my room, and head back down the stairs.

By the door, Mama Sue is standing there with a pair of orange rain boots. She looks as though she's guarding the door or waiting for someone.

"Here, I think these'll probably fit. My granddaughter is about your size."

"How did you know I'd be coming back down so soon?" I ask, shocked at her quick assessment of my poor shoe choice.

"I know a thing or two about a thing or two. You don't get to be my age and not. Now, put these boots on. My granddaughter won't miss 'em."

Mama Sue extends the boots to me, and I graciously take them.

"You have no idea how much help you've already been," I admit. I feel more comfortable with Mama Sue's hospitality than I've ever felt at any hotel.

"Don't mention it. If you need me, I'll be around," she announces and strides back behind the counter with the same smile she greeted me with.

Once I've slipped on the new boots, I open the door, and thankfully, the rain has stopped, but I'm glad to have the boots because they maneuver the mud much better than my Doc Martens.

The Loch Bar & Grill is so close. I see it directly to the left once I've stepped off the concrete slab.

"Well, here goes nothing," I shrug my shoulders and take my leave to the left.

Chapter 4

JAXON

"Fill 'er up, Jax. I ain't exactly a minor," Timothy, one of my younger pack members protests. He might not be a minor, but he's still a young kid. Just barely able to drink.

"Tim, this is your last one. I don't want to have to explain to Kendall why her son is coming home drunk. You're still just a pup," I explain, and he knows I'm right. Tim grew up with his father, which means he didn't shift for the first time until he was 18, when he came to stay with his mother for a full summer.

Kendall was... a loose cannon when she was younger. She had a hot temper, and being a wolf didn't make it any easier. She got into a bar fight years ago, just after she had Tim, and he was sent to live with his father in the city. When Tim turned 18, he came home, and his being around other wolves, it was inevitable. His biology could no longer ignore the shift.

"Ehh... you're probably right. I'll take some water."

I nod my head and pull out a glass from underneath the bar.

"Smart choice."

He takes the glass and begins downing it. From there, I whip around the bar, checking on tables, cleaning them, and doing a sweep to see if there are any other empty tables as the place continues to fill. During the wet season, people shove themselves in here, and I don't mind because it's good for money, which we are sorely needing. I just wish I could afford more help, and that when wet season is over, it stays as steady as it is right now.

I've found myself behind the bar, helping Tina, our bartender make drinks. The door busts open, and I'm mentally calculating a place for whoever has entered a seat. My nose is directed to the door. I've never smelled something so sweet, especially in the rain. It typically covers the scents of others, but the strong and pleasant aroma of lavender and jasmine hit me so hard, I can't ignore it.

My eyes are drawn to the dark-haired beauty making an entrance. Pack members twist in their seats; they're just as drawn to her as I am. My boots carry me to the end of the bar, where I'm almost drooling as the door closes behind her. Her pouty lips make my mouth salivate, and my wolf wants to go near her.

Shhh... settle down, boy, I tell him. He's calling out to her, racing toward the barriers of my mind. I clear my throat as she nears. I turn my head to remove myself from her scent, but it envelops me like blazing fire. I can't ignore her.

As several pack members watch her, my nostrils flare. My eyes pierce theirs, and one by one, they turn away. The woman comes to take a seat at the bar. She's barely tall enough to climb into one of the bar stools, and when she shimmies into her seat, her bountiful breasts jiggle in her cream sweater. She's gorgeous.

I feel rattled in her proximity, speechless even. Yet, I want to be the only one to take her order. She raises her hand, as if she's in a church. What I wouldn't do to worship her.

Wait.

No. She's a stranger, I remind myself.

But, I'm the one to answer her call.

"Welcome to Loch Bar & Grill. Can I start you off with something to drink?" I regurgitate the same greeting I've given to other non-locals since my mind can't seem to process any other words right away.

"Thanks. I'll have a Jack and Coke, and then I'll take the jumbo fried shrimp with french fries. I already memorized my order," she says, a giggle rolling off of her tongue. Her voice is as pleasant as she smells.

"I'll get right on it," I state and quickly turn on my feet to go to the kitchen. I would have run if I wouldn't have looked so stupid doing so.

From the kitchen, through the tiny window, I can see her. She's perfectly content listening to the house music and waiting for her order. She maintains a kind demeanor as she patiently waits. I drop her French fries and jumbo fried shrimp in the deep fryer and come back to make her drink. I pay attention when making her Jack and Coke, wanting it to be strong but not too strong. For some reason, I want her to only have the best.

I return with her drink and place it in front of her with a wrapped straw. She slowly unwraps it and drops it into her drink, and as her lips curl around the straw, my insides begin to melt.

Delicious, my wolf adds. He heavy-foots in a circle, forcing me closer to her.

"You're not from around here?" I say it as more of a statement, though my uptick declares it a question. Speaking to her keeps my wolf at bay, it seems, for now.

"What gave me away?" she asks and looks over the top of her drink, while still taking tiny sips.

"Your jewelry and clothes. It's been a while since I've seen a watch as fancy as the one you're wearing. You're wearing a sweater, and everyone else here is well..."

"Oh God, I'm overdressed?" she laughs, and I can't help but laugh with her.

"No. You're perfect..." my words linger as our eyes meet. The silence between us isn't uncomfortable, though my staring seems to paint her cheeks red. From the kitchen, I hear the baskets float to the top, and I step away to plate her order. I return with her food in hand and several napkins.

"Would you like any sauce with these?"

"Cocktail if you've got it," she adds. I reach underneath the bar and into the mini fridge and pull out a dipping size cup of cocktail sauce and place it next to her plate.

I watch her eat, as if I've never witnessed someone eating before. I witness the pleasure she takes in each bite of her food, and I wish to enjoy her plate the same way she does.

She doesn't seem to mind that I'm watching her. Nor does she look the other way. It's nice to know that I'm all she sees. In a room full of people, she's the only thing I notice.

When she's finished her meal, she pushes her plate forward and pulls out her wallet. I didn't even give her a ticket.

"Let me get your—"

"Don't worry about it. How much could jumbo fried shrimp and fries cost?" she giggles again, and I follow her with a chuckle.

I reach for her card, where her hand is, and when we touch, I feel a spark inside of me. Water from the river surrounding the bar and grill fills my lungs, and I almost lose my balance. I see the two of us, running through the woods, her raven hair flowing in the wind. Me, by her side, running to catch up to her. Her smile is as refreshing as a quenching glass of water, and I can't assume anything but the obvious.

Mine, my wolf states the inevitable, and I'm shaken. A human? How could this be?

"Is everything okay?" she implores, standing up on the bar stool and leaning over the bar. I slowly find my balance and remove my hand from hers.

"Yeah," I run my fingers through my hair as I allow the realization to hit me. "Haven't eaten today. I'm okay," I lie and quickly step toward the cash register. I ring up her order and place her card in the car reader.

I'm curious about my mysterious mate who's just blown into town. With her name on her card, I don't have to wonder her name, though when I see it, my eyes squint in disbelief.

"Mira Jefferson?"

"Yes?" she responds as though she's innocent, and I can't be more upset. My wolf is begging me to calm down, though I cannot. She didn't come for a meal; she came to talk about buying up my business.

"I'm Jaxon, Jaxon Coolidge."

Her eyes show recognition, and she smirks. The audacity.

"Well, you said to come in person. Here I am." Her tone is absolute, and I'm conflicted. I can't believe this outsider is my mate.

"Indeed, I did, though I didn't think you'd leave your polished palace long enough to come and see about your own personal business."

"Excuse me?"

"You heard me," I retort and place her card back onto the bar, taking several steps backward.

"I did exactly as requested, and for your information, I don't live in a polished palace. Far from it," she corrects, though I'm doubtful. From the Gucci tag on her jeans, I can tell she's not struggling.

"Sure, Gucci girl. Those jeans probably cost a fortune," I point out, my arms instinctively folding over my chest.

"They were on sale. Why am I telling you that? Listen, I didn't come here to argue. I'm here to help you out. Your father—"

"My father and I are not the same people. You came here to assess the business. I'm no fool. Offering me money to buy out this place doesn't hold the same merit with me as it did my father. I'm guessing since he didn't go through with the deal, either something wasn't right with it, or he chose to fight through his financial troubles. I might do the same." My shoulders shrug as her head twists from side to side, as though I've said something wrong.

"Well, your father is an idiot for not taking the offer—"

Anger boils up inside me in response to that. "My father is dead!" I roar, much louder than I meant to. Now, all eyes are on us, and I can see the remorse immediately clouding her eyes.

"I-I'm sorry, Jaxon, I had no idea." She sounds sincere, and I know she was unaware. I did not disclose my father's death, only that I'd be taking over the business during our voicemail exchanges.

"Listen, you asked me to come in person to make the offer. I'm here to do that. Why don't we set up a time to talk?"

"I think you should just leave," I grit out, my tone is firm and unmovable.

Mira doesn't say another word. She takes her card and her receipt and leaves the bar, stomping my heart as she goes.

Chapter 5

Mira

Those were literally the best jumbo shrimp I've ever had in my life, but my meal was ruined by Jaxon's attitude. I truly came to do what he'd asked me to do. What Mr. Sanderson asked me to do. I don't care, personally one way or the other, the place could be a dump. Mr. Sanderson knows what he's doing, and any time he acquires a piece of real estate, it's for a reason. I was truly hungry, and it just happened to work out that I would run into the boss on my first visit.

But, he's an asshole. A handsome asshole. But an asshole nonetheless. His scruffy beard gives him sex appeal, and his beautiful canine-like teeth make his smile sharp and daring. The way his baby blue eyes penetrated my own made my legs quiver.

Not quiver. Yes, quiver. I don't know.

Today is clearly not the day to talk business, and I'll need to strategize if I'm going to even get close to him again. Now that he knows who I am, he'll be on high alert when I enter his establishment again.

Racing down the marina dock, I return to Mama Sue's, stomping and no doubt trekking muddy boot prints into the lobby.

"What's got you scowlin'?" Mama Sue leans over the counter, looking me over.

I take a deep breath, and the only words that come through my lips are, "Jaxon Coolidge." His name tastes like poison on my tongue.

Mama Sue laughs. A full head toss laugh, and it confuses me. Does she know something I don't? Did I say something funny and don't realize it?

"I'm sorry, sweetheart. I don't mean to laugh. He has a lot on his plate. He's not quite... himself these days," she admits, and for some reason, the mystery in what that means intrigues me. I step closer to the counter and wait to see if she'll say more. She rises to her full height, which is around the same as me, 5'5 or so, and she folds her arms over her chest, releasing an exhale.

"See, Jaxon was a good mechanic. He had dreams of opening his own shop but his daddy's passing took all that from him. He had to take over the bar and grill. Well, I suppose he didn't have to, but it was his daddy's dying wish you see. He had to stop living his own life to assume his father's, in more ways than one." I'm not sure what the last part completely means, but it seems silly to me to be this flustered over no longer being a mechanic.

"Was fixing cars better than owning an established restaurant? Was he fixing luxury cars or motorcycles?" I query, hoping to gain a little more clarity on the subject.

Mama Sue responds, "Well, it's not just that. Jaxon also did… community outreach, and to him, that was something better. It made him more involved."

"Involved? The man who just told me to get out does not seem like the community caring type," I express, my mouth twisting in disbelief.

"Don't be fooled by his harsh tone. Jax's a good boy. Always has been."

"That might be so, but I've been sent here to acquire his business, and I only have 7 days to do it in. He asked me to come and make him an offer in person, but now that I'm here... well, he kicked me out once he knew who I was."

Mama Sue nods her head and then places her hand on top of mine. She gives it a loving squeeze, and then a word of advice.

"Be persistent. Be genuine, and use all 7 days, baby. Because you're gonna need them."

That doesn't sound very reassuring. Mama Sue taps my hand, and that feels like my cue to head to my room. On the way up the stairs, my deadline is screaming in my head. If I don't get him to agree, I can kiss my promotion goodbye. The "*good life*" that Jaxon thinks I live, will really be more than nothing but a dream.

Chapter 6

JAXON

Since Mira's exit, I've had a mind-searing headache. My wolf is pleading with me to bond with her, but I need more information. This just doesn't seem probable. If there has ever been any record of a wolf and human mating, I will need to check with the record keeper. She'd be the only person who would know the information of that magnitude. It wouldn't be widespread throughout the packs. The alphas would want that kept secret. Otherwise, our bloodline would be filled with impurities. Not that there's anything wrong with humans, but they lack the compassion and understanding it would take to understand a shifter. Unless she's a witch, but even then, witches are still human at their core.

After Tina and Brody, the cook, leave, I lock up for the evening and head toward the forest in search of answers. Her scent still lingers, the rain paints her location in the direction of Mama Sue's. She's safe there until I can figure out what the hell is going on.

I breach the edge of the forest, and when I'm certain no one is around, I allow my body to shift. It's no longer painful but a feeling I welcome. The first few shifts are horrible, but they're seamless and connected once you get the hang of it.

My fur is the first to appear. Up my arms and on my legs. My clothes rip into shreds as my body takes on my wolf form. The bones in my back adjust, grow and stretch to accommodate my wolf's physique.

My snout picks up on Mira's scent once more before I burst forward, racing through the woods. My mind's eye is settled on Mira and will not rest until I'm given answers. I crisscross through the trees, passing the pack's living grounds to the edge of our land where the record keeper lives.

My fear is that mating with a human could be fatal to her and to me. When a wolf loses its mate, it never mates again. Shifters have long life spans, and a human will die long before I will. I would be crushed. Though we have a human form, we were once just wolves until the packs began being killed off by other supernatural creatures and humans. A witch, a friend to the wolves, blessed us. She gave us her magic that created shifters so that we could live full lives without being hunted to the ends of the earth while remaining true to our birth heritage. We can survive in either form while maintaining certain wolf aspects in our human form, though we are not technically human.

At the edge of the woods, where our land meets the creek, the record keeper's home sits quietly and undisturbed. I haven't been here since the day I became alpha and was given the knowledge of the previous alphas. She won't be happy to see me. She doesn't care for visitors.

I shift into my human form when I reach her doorstep, though she can communicate telepathically, she doesn't prefer to do so.

There is a pair of jeans for me in the right barrel outside of her home. She keeps them for the wolves, as she does not want to see our naked bodies. The women's barrel contains shirts and pants, since they have more to cover. Once dressed, I knock three times and wait for her response. Her candles are lit, and I know she's awake. The old woman hardly sleeps these days.

"Alpha," she says when she approaches the door. She does not invite me in, but she doesn't turn me away.

"Celine, may I come in? I have an... issue to discuss with you," I whisper. I do not want others who might be lurking to hear.

"An issue... with whom?" her aged eyes squint, and she leans into the door frame, unbothered by my tone or request.

"I have a question about a possible record. Celine, can I please come in?" I repeat. I only ask out of respect. As the alpha, I'm allowed anywhere on our land, though I don't like to bully my way into other people's spaces.

"I suppose. Don't complain about the smell... I'm making fish for dinner," she says and slides across the floor, allowing me entrance. I smelled the fish when I approached her home; I'm not bothered by the scent of fish. The restaurant is on the water for wolf's sake.

"Have a seat and get on with your question. I'd like to eat sometime tonight," she mumbles, and I huff in frustration. This woman can be tiresome, but she's a quintessential part of our pack.

"I'll make this as simple as possible. I found my mate today. Rather, she found me, but she's a human. How could that be possible?"

"I see your dilemma. Put your mind at rest; your mate is no human," Celine affirms, yet I don't feel reassured.

"How can you truly know? She's in her late 20's, she would have shifted by now. I would have scented her wolf."

"Not if her wolf hasn't yet been awakened. If she never caught the fever, her wolf is lying dormant. Just like Timothy. Perhaps she wasn't raised by wolves. You would have scented them also," she points out, and she's right. Had she been around other wolves, I would have smelled them on her. From the moment she entered the restaurant, all I smelled... was her.

"What can I do then, to find out if she is indeed a wolf? Should I go to her? Spend more time with her?"

"If you can, just be careful. Remember, the fever is difficult even with a pack and support. Some of us are not strong enough to undergo the change, especially the older we get," she distantly mentions. Her eyes drift to the window, where the trees rustle and blades of grass blow. She hasn't shifted in close to a decade. She's reaching the end of her life span, but I know she misses running. The same way I will when my time comes.

I'd forgotten that some do not survive the first shift, it has been a long time since that has occurred. I wouldn't let that happen to Mira, even if she was trying to see what the restaurant was worth. That would be a fate worse than death for the both of us. Knowing my mate without ever truly knowing her would kill me, and letting her die would be even worse.

"I understand, Celine. Thank you. I will not keep you. Enjoy your evening."

"And you, alpha. Go to your mate and keep a watchful eye on her. I fear things will get worse before they get better."

Her statement is more menacing than I'd hoped, but it puts the fire under me that I need in order to find out more about Mira. Who she truly is and where she came from.

Chapter 7

Mira

Waking up feeling hungover is scary when you're not actually hungover. I'm in desperate need of coffee this morning. My feet hit the ground like a pound of bricks. I'm weighed down from the stresses of the previous day, though I had an amazing night's rest. It's probably all the rain, I convince myself.

I detect the smell of coffee, and it points me in the direction of downstairs. I trek my feet across the room, open the door and make my way toward the glorious coffee. I know I look like I just got hit by a truck because I haven't taken the time to comb out my wavy tresses or even wipe the sleep out of my eyes.

Cooffeee... I feel like a zombie as I make my way down the stairs. I'm underdressed, for the first time ever, wearing my two-piece pink and white satin pajama set, where others are already fully dressed. It's barely 6 a.m. There are several people downstairs, standing around conversing. There are eyes on me, but none of the stares are rude or unwanted. They're followed by smiles, which warrants one from me.

There's a line in front of the coffee pot. That's fine, I can wait. It gives me time to check out the setup. When it's my turn, I grab one of the wide mouth coffee cups and make a full pour. I need it if I'm going to figure out what to do about Jaxon. As of today, I only have six days.

As I continue to travel the line to the creamers and sugar, I'm put off by the fact that my favorite creamers aren't here. There's just a regular, non-flavored one. This will have to do for now. A regular cup of coffee is better than no cups of coffee.

After stirring in my creamer, I spin on my heels, and I run into a very strong and firm chest.

"Oof..." the wind is practically knocked out of me, and my coffee tilts from my drink just a smidge.

"Excuse me—" I begin saying until I realize I've run into the object of my frustration. "Oh, it's you," I add, my eyes not being able to keep themselves from rolling.

Jaxon runs his hand over his face and blinks, as though he's trying to rid himself of something. He places his hand on my arm gently and guides me away from the other people in the lobby. I'm almost inclined to not allow him to do so, but there's something about his touch that feels... soft and familiar.

He pulls me away from prying eyes, and into the center of an open walkway where we're alone and secluded.

"I need to apologize to you," he starts and rubs his hand over his face again. Perhaps he has some sort of anxiety issue, since he's done this more than once.

"Oh really, for what?" I know exactly what he needs to apologize for. I'm just hoping that he doesn't think that simply saying he needs to apologize will suffice.

He smirks, his grin is wide and Cheshire like, but his smile is hypnotizing.

"I'm sorry for the way I acted yesterday. I have a lot on my plate, and I really meant no harm. Though I can understand how it could be perceived another way. I hope you'll forgive me."

The straightness of his face worries me. I know people who lie through their teeth and never blink. Perhaps his apology isn't sincere, and we don't need to be this personal with one another anyway.

"I understand. I'll come by later and we can try to open a discussion about your restaurant." I keep my statement short and twist to head back to my room. I'm nearing the stairs when I feel the wind shift my way and footsteps coming toward me from behind. Choosing to ignore them, I take to the stairs where I'm stopped again by Jaxon. He's touching my elbow this time, and it sends chills up my spine.

"I'd like to discuss the restaurant; why don't you come by tonight around 8 for a late dinner and we can talk some more about the terms?" His thick eyebrows furrow toward the center of his face, and there's a grin trembling in the corner of his mouth. I want to say no, that we can discuss things at a reasonable hour, during lunch.

This sounds like a date, *which might not be so bad*. Wait, what am I thinking?

"If I'm going to sell the place, I have questions that need to be answered before I can make a decision," he says in the wake of my hesitancy, and I don't want to push him away any further. If I do, that could be the end of my promotion before I ever even get it.

His hand is still touching my elbow, and I'm in no rush to make him move, but as familiar as I feel with Jaxon, something about him also seems off. It could just be his reaction to me showing up yesterday.

Giving in will have to do, and it will hopefully put me closer to what I'm trying to achieve.

"Alright, I'll meet you there. We can discuss business and hopefully, you can gain some clarity on the situation."

"I'd love that."

The way Jaxon's tongue flutters when he says love makes my thighs squeeze together, and I know then I have to get away from him.

"Alright, I'll see you at 8," I confirm and pull away from him, almost taking off into a sprint back to my room. As soon as the door closes, I release the breath I didn't know I was holding and take a seat on the bed. The coffee I'd wanted so badly, now I have no desire to drink. My mind is racing with possibilities and thoughts I'm not ready to render myself to thinking about.

I place my coffee on the nightstand beside my bed and lay back down. I still feel hungover and a little more rest couldn't hurt. I didn't even drink the night before, but the oncoming headache pressing its way to the front of my mind said otherwise.

It's easy for me to fall back into the comfortable bed and find sleep. My breathing slows almost immediately, and I fall into dreamland...

"Please don't leave me, please," I plead and kiss the wolf's amber fur. His body trembles underneath my touch, and I lean into him, hovering over his body. I hold onto him as tightly as humanly possible, but I'm not strong enough to keep him with me. Tears rush from my eyes as my beautiful wolf shifts one last time.

His fur becomes rough olive skin. His snout becomes a human nose with a chiseled jaw line and handsome scruff. His large and alert ears now rest comfortably on the side of his head, and my once alive wolf is now an unalive human...

Several hours later, when I wake up, I'm drenched in sweat, and my pulse is racing. I have never made it that far in the dream before, and I've never seen the wolf shift... ever. I'm also unfamiliar with the human face of the man. It wasn't specific, just the lower part of his face was clear, and it could belong to anyone.

If I didn't know any better, I'd think my dreams were trying to tell me something, but what? What could there possibly be for me to find out about a supernatural creature that does not exist?

Last night was the first night I didn't dream of the wolf. Yet, I did dream I was in a forest, running through it barefoot. Today, I dream of my wolf becoming human.

It's stress, I tell myself. I've been stressed for far too long and my imagination is taking on a life of its own. I need to hurry and get whatever this is with Jaxon out of the way, and then I'll be relieved of my largest burden so that I can move forward.

Sometimes not reaching the heights we strive to reach can be more stressful than we realize, and receiving this promotion is something I've strived toward for so long. It's no wonder I'm having crazy dreams.

I've made up an excuse to tell myself, but deep down, in my core, I know there's more to these dreams than I'm willing to let myself believe right now.

Chapter 8

JAXON

"Your mate, huh? I'm waiting for the day it happens to me. I'll admit, I was starting to believe you'd be a lone wolf forever," Pike laughs, and though I don't like his joke, I agree. I'm 30, and most wolves find their mates early in life. At times, in their teens. I gave up hope that there was someone out there for me, and now to find out pants to possess her, though I know rightfully she's mine.

"There's more I need to find out about her, but I'm positive she's the one. My wolf saw it; we felt it."

I'm wiping down the tables before Mira comes in. It's been a long day. Before I set up for dinner with Mira, I needed to talk to someone about what Celine told me.

She wasn't much of a conversationalist anyway, and Pike isn't just my beta but also my best friend.

"Well, find out and don't be afraid to let yourself. If she's as perfect as you say—"

"Oh, I never said she was perfect," I correct. "I also don't know much about her to know how compatible we are, but it doesn't work that way, does it? We're naturally supposed to be compatible, but we're butting heads because of the business."

"The business that you don't even want to run? The business that you would secretly be happy to be rid of?" Pike's left eyebrow raises as though he's pointing something out to me that I didn't already know.

"Pike, you don't get it. The restaurant is a burden, true, but I'm conflicted. My responsibilities as the alpha and to the restaurant are overwhelming. Even with you helping to take care of the pack, that doesn't rid me of the guilt I feel for not being able to do more for them. That's the problem I'm facing. If I sell the business, I'll have more money and I can focus on the pack, sure. This place helps to keep some of our members out of trouble and gives them somewhere to go. It's a money pit, but it's saved a lot of lies too," I admit, and this is the first time

I've ever said it out loud. When my dad was alive, I had a totally different outlook, but now, being the person to run the business on my own, I can't also forget about the pack. Now, with Mira in the picture, I just don't know how everything fits or what decision I should be making.

"I have no problem doing anything for the pack. Pack is family, and I'll do anything to protect the family. Which brings me to the reason why I'm glad you called. I know you don't think there's anything out there, but I've been out there more than you recently. I can feel the disturbance. I see things that are out of place. It's not my job, as your beta, to question your judgment. It is my job, though, as your best and only real friend, to tell you that I see you're overwhelmed, but this also needs your attention, brother."

Pike's eyes are narrowed and intense, which means he's serious. He's a bit more emotional than most, but that's part of what makes him special. Pike and I were raised closely; our fathers were best friends and so were our mothers. My mother died just a year after giving birth to me. She was always a bit sick after she shifted the first time. Her body kept trying to reject the shift, and it eventually caught up to her.

Pike's mother followed just six short years later when there was an attack on the pack by a neighboring enemy. She was strong but unfortunately fell in battle. Pike's father never forgave himself for the way she died, and he drank himself into oblivion, which took years to do. He eventually shifted one day and ran off. We haven't seen him since.

My dad stepped in and raised him, and we've been together our entire lives. He's just a year younger than me, though at times, he acts fifteen years older. He's the more level-headed one at times, and without him, I don't know where I would be. Naturally, I'm alpha because my father was, but if I could have chosen, I would have chosen Pike. He was better suited for the job, and then I could run the restaurant, while Pike was alpha. That's just wishful thinking that was never going to happen, though.

"I hear you, Pike. Tonight, once I'm done with Mira, you and I will go out and investigate together. Give me a few hours. I'll text you when we're wrapping up here."

I give him a nod, and his face relaxes. I never wanted him to think I wasn't taking him seriously, but with everything else going on, it's been hard to dedicate my full attention to whatever he thinks might be out there.

"Thank you, brother. Thank you."

Before Pike leaves, I clap him on the back, showing my support, and hang the closed sign outside the door. Although, I've been spreading the word all day that I wouldn't be open past 6:30 tonight because I needed time to prepare. Once I'm satisfied with the arrangement of the tables and chairs, that I stacked against the walls there's only one table left with two chairs in the center of the floor. I completely decorated it with a candle stick, proper silverware that I Googled for proper placement, and a tablecloth, that just happened to be in the kitchen thankfully, I go into the bathroom to change my clothes.

I could have lived here. There is an apartment above the restaurant that I use from time to time, but it reminds me too much of my dad, so I only briefly used it to shower before Pike arrived. Now in the bathroom, I unzip my gym bag that contains a new pair of jeans, a white and blue striped button up flannel, that a woman at the Walmart mentioned matched my eyes, and my cleanest pair of boots.

Dressing from top to bottom, I've chosen to leave my shirt unbuttoned enough so that I don't feel stuck inside my shirt. My hair could use some type of styling I suppose but that's not me. I run my hands underneath the water faucet and then finger comb my hair back away from my face. This will have to do.

The clock on the wall attracts my attention. It's ten till 8, and I haven't heard a word from Mira all day. I don't know why I'm expecting to. This isn't a traditional meal, I suppose.

As the clock ticks down, I find myself checking small things, wanting everything to be perfect for her arrival. At the last minute, I remember the candles I purchased earlier and decide to light them. I'm thankful at this moment I don't let people smoke in here, but the smell of fish from the marina and daily cooking can stink the place up a bit.

Simultaneously as I light the last candle, I scent Mira approaching the dock. A minute or so later, she's at the door, peeking in, like she'd rather see me before I see her. I'm tucked over in the corner near the bar, so she can't see me. I'll give her, her wish and wait for her to see me before I go over to the door.

After several seconds, she knocks, and I enter her eye view. Her face twitches like she wants to smile but won't allow herself to. I close the distance between the bar and the door in three bounds, and then realize my hands are sweating. Perhaps I didn't think this completely through.

Let her in, my wolf reminds me, and he puts me back on track with my mission. I lean in and open the door, and my mouth is just short of the floor when she enters with a trench coat on. The only thing I can see are her rain boots, her large purse that she's carrying on her arm, and dark pant legs, but only from the ankle down. Her hair is pulled up into a high ponytail which gives me the perfect view of her face. Her eyes are amber and wide set. She has this way of always looking like she knows more than she's ready to say.

"Can I take your coat?"

"S-sure," she answers, and I politely spin her around to help her remove her coat. As she lets it fall into my arms, her top is exposed, and it's a tight fitted v-neck long-sleeved shirt that gives me a full show of her heavy breasts.

Mira turns around, and I quickly raise my eyes to where they should be, hoping she doesn't catch my inappropriateness.

"So, I brought the paperwork. I think honestly, now that I've personally seen the place, you could ask for more money. If it were—"

"Mira, let me ask you a question. Where did you go to college?" I ask, redirecting the conversation. I could truly care less about figures tonight. I want to, no, I need to know more about her. She stops speaking for a moment, and her face holds a shocked expression. I reach for her hand and lead her over to the table and pull out her chair. She takes a seat, where I place her jacket on the back of her seat, and she waits for me to take mine. When I do, it seems she's found her voice again.

"Middle Tennessee. I wanted to stay close to my parents," she explains with hesitance. Her eyes are squinted closely. She's trying to figure out where this is going.

"I see. I've visited Murfreesboro a time or two to fix a few cars up there for a guy I know who owns a dealership. Where about did you grow up?

Mira looks around as I ask my question. She scans the room, like she's waiting for something or someone to jump out. When it's apparent she's done looking, her eyes study me, and I do my best not to smile.

"Do you think this is a date, Jaxon?" her voice shrills in the small space. I'm not sure if she's surprised or upset, as her face gives me no clues.

"I don't think this is a date. I think—"

"Let me tell you something, *Jaxon,* I would NEVER date someone like you. And I mean never," she repeats, and I'm not sure what to make of that, but I'm extremely offended.

"And why is that, city girl?" I retort and fold my arms, waiting for her to respond, and when she does, she doesn't speak as casually as I just did.

Mira jumps to her feet and hits her hands on the table, her open hands are as red as the blood pumping through her veins.

"You don't know me, Jaxon, but you think you do. Yes, I grew up in the city, but it's Nashville; not New York. Yes, I was probably given certain opportunities that you weren't, but I can't do anything about who my parents are and what they afforded me. But rest assured, everything I have, I busted my ass for it. Nothing was ever given to me! Stop judging me you country hick!"

she shouts, and her chest heaves like she's just run a mile. I suppose her lips did.

"Why don't you get your pretty and privileged ass out of my bar before you bust a blood vessel." I nod my head toward the front door, in case she's forgotten where it is.

Her mouth pops open in shock, but my stance is unmovable. Mira huffs, and I can almost taste the frustration spewing from her mouth. Her nostrils flare, and if she were a dragon, she'd be breathing fire.

Mira doesn't say another word, and I'm not inclined to do so either. She kicks her chair to the side, clearing her path and grabs her coat. She doesn't bother putting it back on, nor does she give me a last look. Mira opens the door and then slams it so hard, I feel the building shake. That could just be in my mind.

One thing is for certain; if she's not a wolf, she's got a temper just like one. Mira leaving early is of her own devices. She has no reason to be so snooty. I'm not judgmental, I'm just observant. She's calling it how she thinks she sees it and I'm doing the same.

She wasn't wrong; I was attempting to turn this into a date. She's my mate, and I wanted to see her as a person instead of the enemy I'd first become acquainted with. I can't make her be nice to me, and I won't bow down to her just because she's my mate. Though my wolf has other thoughts and feelings entirely. He runs in my mind, beating against the very fabric that holds us together. He's upset, but he will yield to me. Mira has made her decision, for now. That she would never date a country hick. But she has no idea that she won't be "dating" me; she'll be mine forever. Once I figure out the conundrum of this situation.

The only upside to her leaving early is that I can investigate Pike's suspicions a little sooner than I'd planned.

Chapter 9

Mira

What an ASS. Jaxon is the sexiest, rudest, most judgmental person I've ever met, and that's why I won't date him. He's convinced that he knows me so well, yet he knows nothing about me, nor where I come from. Yes, I've been blessed in my life. I would be a liar to say that I haven't, however, I've had my fair share of downfalls, broken relationships, not to mention failures.

He doesn't know me, but I've been dealing with people like him all my life. I've always been underestimated and taken for granted. People see what they want to see, even though I know who I am and what I have to offer, and even what I've been through. I'm a bit sensitive and don't want to be told who or what I am because I'm the only person who knows who that is. If only I could convince myself of that.

Trekking through the mud, Jaxon's smug face keeps appearing in my mind, and my stomach is touching my back because I'm starving. I didn't wake up on time to begin with, and by the time I finally got ready, I couldn't decide on what to wear, like it was important. I'm so glad I didn't wear something cuter, or I would be even angrier than I am right now.

Mama Sue's door swings open, and a couple comes out together. They're holding hands, smiling at one another. I long for the simplicity of a relationship, of someone to depend on, but it's never that easy. Otherwise, I'd be happily coupled.

I pass the couple on the way in and am thankful when I find a basket of rolls and fried chicken on the edge of the table in the cafeteria. My intestines can literally taste the food that I'm desperate to dunk in my mouth.

Like a child who's sneaking sweets, I pick up a plate and pile on three chicken legs and two rolls. I can hardly wait to get to my room to start downing them. On the staircase, I start on my first chicken leg, and by the time

I've made it inside of my room, I'm ready to start on the second.

Ten or so minutes later, I've taken my entire plate down. It's completely worth it when I'm so full I barely have the energy to take my clothes off. I bend over, in an attempt to remove my shoes, but I start to feel lightheaded. My hands firmly plant themselves on the ground, but my stomach rumbles like boots in a dryer. It has been a while since I've eaten like that, but I was starving. It's probably just because I ate too fast.

Taking long deep breaths, I feel more stable, so I stand up to remove my clothes. The moment I reach my full vertical state, the lightheadedness returns, and my stomach starts to cramp. It's not time for my cycle. I shouldn't be showing signs this early.

The only thing I can do to make myself feel better is lie down. It wouldn't be the first time I laid in bed with a full day's clothes on. As soon as my head hits the pillow, I begin writhing in pain again. I grab at my stomach, hoping to hold myself together, but I feel like I'm coming undone. Sweat beads and pools at my temples, and now I'm concerned I've eaten something contaminated. This feels almost like food poisoning, though I've never gotten a headache with food poisoning, and I've had that more times than I'm pleased to admit. Something is very wrong.

When I was a child, no matter the problem, the only person who has ever been able to make me feel better was my mother. I haven't even spoken to her since I made it to this Podunk town. She'll give me my space, but I know she's probably worried sick.

With the little strength I do have, I pull my phone from my pocket and dial my mom's number. Only two rings pass before she picks up.

"Oh sweetheart, I'm so happy you called. I told Dad not to worry," she says, with a slight hint of worry in her own voice.

"Did you? That's interesting considering you're worried currently," I tease and wince in pain that I try to keep quiet. Mom can still comfort me without knowing that I need the comfort.

"That's my job as a mom. The worries never stop, ever. What are you doing, sweetheart? Resting?" Mom questions. She's a genius and will know if I'm lying, so I won't attempt to.

"I am resting, but I'm not feeling well. I think the chicken I ate downstairs might have been bad. It had been sitting out, but I don't know for how long," I mention, thinking back to when I left Mama Sue's and if I saw the chicken then. I can't remember.

"Well sweetheart, you've always had a bit of a sensitive stomach. Need I remind you about the eighth grade dance?" she snickers, and I'm in too much pain to laugh, but she's right.

"Don't even bring it up. But you're right, Mom. Maybe I should see about getting some Ginger Ale to see if my stomach will calm down then."

"Ginger Ale and a roll of crackers has always worked. Go ahead and get what you need and call me when you get a chance. Just check in so me and Dad don't worry as much, okay?"

Her voice is pleading, and I'd do anything to make her happy. "I will, Mom. I love you."

"I love you, too, sweetheart," she says and ends the call. I place my phone onto the nightstand and lay my head against my pillow. The moonlight catches my attention as it beams across the wall, and when I turn to face it, I hear what sounds like a growling howl coming from the trees.

The sound of the wolf calls to something deep inside of me, and I can't ignore it. Slowly and as carefully as possible, I toddle to the window to look out of it, hoping to see where the howl came from. I don't spot them right away, but after a few minutes, I notice a set of glowing yellow eyes amongst the trees. I hone in on them, and at the same time, a wave of nausea comes over me.

My hand grips my shirt, and I place my other hand against the wall, but neither does anything to hold me steady. My vision becomes blurry, and my head throbs with pain. Before I can steady myself again, or try to, I fall to the ground, and the room around me goes black.

Chapter 10

Jaxon

Go left, now! I send a command in Pike's direction. I hate to admit it, but he was right. A lone wolf is out here, roaming around near our pack, and I can briefly hear his thoughts. He means us harm. As he weaves in and out of the trees, I aim to block his pathway to an escape by trapping him dead in the center. Either way he goes, he will have to face me or Pike. I have not laid eyes on him completely, though I've caught traces of his scent and blips of his darkened fur. He's fast; I must give him that.

Pike goes left, and I swing right, hoping to make the lone wolf trap himself in the center, but he's cunning. Instead of racing away from us, he lets us speed ahead of him. I hear his howl of success coming from behind us now. He tricked us.

Fuck. My thoughts rage as Pike and I meet in the center of the forest, where we would have met the omega had he been stupid enough to follow us into the trap.

He's smart, fast, and he knows our home. He has to be found.

We'll find him, Jax. Trust me. On my life and the pack, we will.

I know. I'm sorry, brother. I should have listened to you.

We can't worry about that now, Jaxon. We need to inform the pack.

The pack. The thought of alerting them to a wandering threat concerned me. They might not take it well. Again, with so much change and instability there was a lot to worry about, and I hadn't been where I should be. Right here with my family. I feel more than ever that I've neglected them.

Together, Pike and I scamper through the forest back to the pack. I linger behind him to make sure the omega hasn't followed us back, and when I'm certain I can't sense him or hear his thoughts, I enter the pack's grounds.

There are children laughing, cubs playing. Water magic is being displayed for the elders to judge their skills. Everyone in our pack has a gift and can manipulate water through that gift. Mine is being able to call water to me in large amounts. I can manipulate something as large as the lake. Pike can create weapons out of water; he's skilled and a showoff.

Some of the elders of our tribe are cooking; I can smell the spit roast roasting something hearty. This is home, and this is my family. A lone wolf can be a very dangerous one, especially one who wants revenge. Through the omega's thoughts, I heard whispers of murder, rage, revenge, and starting over. These are all the makings of something terrible to come.

I'm greeted as I stroll through the evening rituals of my pack. I smile, yet my heart is heavy. Several cubs run around my legs. I would typically play with them, but not now. In front of my cabin, I take my human form and slide into a pair of rugged jeans and a t-shirt, Pike at my side, but still in wolf form. He really should have been alpha.

Pack Loch! Gather around! The alpha has news!

Pike releases his command, and instinctively, the pack gathers around my cabin, huddling up so they can hear what I have to say. A heavy sigh finds its way out of me before I begin, and the weight of losing my father hangs over me like dead weight. He would know exactly what to do, and he would have caught the omega tonight. I should have listened to Pike, and I could only hope that my negligence wouldn't be consequential to the pack.

"Tonight, Pike and I chased an omega from our lands. It was Pike who first sensed him, his presence. This lone wolf has been penetrating our lands for the last two weeks. He wants blood; he wants revenge. I heard that much of his thoughts. I'm not sure of on who, if he has a vendetta, or if this is random. What I know is he's smart, and he's dangerous.

"Starting tonight, we will set up a security detail at the north and south perimeters of our lands in order to keep everyone safe. Pike will choose who is best suited for the detail. As alpha, it is my responsibility to see to it that this gets handled, and it is my word that it will be."

I brace for impact, for some type of bite back or disrespect. I anticipate the questions that will come about whether I can keep them safe, if I am the alpha my father was. Yet, they do not come.

"Yes, alpha."

"Glad to hear it!"

"Ain't no lone wolf takin' down Pack Loch!"

I'm surprised at the members of the pack. Their support truly is unwavering.

You think too much, Pike's accusation is a truth I don't want to admit. I can block people from hearing my thoughts, but I've never been able to keep him out for some reason. He's the only person who can hear me when I don't want them to and read me when I'd prefer for them not to be able to.

Shut up. Can you take care of this? I have to get back to the bar and grill to prepare for tomorrow. It's—

Saturday, I know. Go ahead. I'll take care of it and set up the detail. I'll check in with you in the morning.

Pike and I nod at one another and I grab a quick change of clothes to take back to the bar. Saturdays and Sundays are my busiest days at the bar & grill, and if I don't open, there will be people who don't eat, including those at Mama Sue's, which means Mira.

I'm angry with her, but I don't want her to starve.

I toss on a pair of socks and boots before heading out and grab my jacket from the porch swing, and take off into the woods. My mind is thick with thoughts of frustration and worry. For the first time ever, I have to admit that I might be a little tired. I typically don't feel worn out, but I am feeling it now. Since commemorating Dad's body back to the lake, I have been tired and racing against myself. Once this omega is caught and I figure things out with Mira, I'm overdue for a few days off.

Heading back into town, my stomach starts to tighten. There's something gnawing at my gut, and it makes me double over. I stumble, breaking my fall by grabbing a tree. My wolf growls... no, he's whimpering. He's in pain, and so am I.

Mate, he says, and I feel it too. My body is being pulled in the direction of Mama Sue's. One foot at a time, I move through the pain and push myself toward the edge of town. The closer I get to her, the more pain I feel. Her scent is covered in musk... I can almost taste her perspiration.

Mama Sue's seems quiet enough, and the lights are low except for in the lobby. I burst through the front door, and Mama Sue looks over at me.

"Mira," I say, almost wincing. Her face twists, yet she does not protest my request.

"Second floor, first door off the shoulder." Mama Sue points to the staircase and I take off, jumping two stairs at a time until I get to Mira's door. I twist the knob, and thankfully it's unlocked.

When I see her huddled up against the wall, her eyes shut, and sweat beads covering her body, I realize she's caught the fever. As her body trembles, I descend to the floor, rip off my jacket, pull her into my lap, and stroke the sweat away from her already very pale face. She's got the fever, but her skin is cold to the touch. That's actually a good sign.

"You'll be okay, my little wolf. You'll be okay." I leave kisses around her temples and hope that soon she'll wake up, and I'll be able to explain.

Chapter 11

MIRA

I'm so warm and comfortable when my eyes open. My vision is blurry, but I know I'm in my room. Then it hits me. I'm in my room, but there's someone's arms around me. I look slightly under my lids and see two very strong arms surrounding me. The arms lead up to very broad and wide shoulders, connected to a thick, olive neck. His blonde hair gives him completely away. His eyes are shut, and his breathing is slow.

What happened?

I begin recollecting the night's events, and I remember the chicken dinner. Mom's conversation. Passing out on the floor. Wait... howling, then passing out on the floor.

What is he doing in my room?

My mind begins to race, yet I feel whole in Jaxon's arms, unafraid even.

I clear my throat, hoping it will be enough to wake him up. It is, and when his baby blues peep down at me, I inwardly melt.

"How are you feeling?" he asks, his voice husky with sleep.

"I... I think I'm okay. I think I might have a slight stomach flu. Wh-what are you doing here?" It's a valid question, even if he is possibly the reason I'm feeling better.

Jaxon scoots up on the headboard a little, his arms bringing me with him.

"You're... sick, in a sense. I was worried about you and came to check on you. When you didn't answer the door, I began to worry, and your door was unlocked. Lucky, I came in when I did."

His eyes are shifty. It feels like a lie, but I don't get the sense he'd actually do anything bad to me.

"I see. Well," I start, and attempt to get up, but when I do, the headache slaps me again, and I'm forced back into his arms.

"I wouldn't try that right now if I were you. I'm gonna call Mama Sue and ask her to bring up some of the soup she made," he adds, and I'm wondering when Mama Sue made soup. Outside, it's still dark, so I guess I haven't been out that long.

"What time is it?" I question, doing my best to look over his large arm to see the clock by my bedside, but it's no use. He's too big. Not that it's a complaint.

"It's 2 a.m."

My eyes bulge with confusion. "How long was I out?" Panic rolls over me, but the second I feel nervous, Jaxon pulls me against his chest and rubs his hand over my hair, stroking it. His touch comforts me instantly, and I lie against him, deciding not to fight his comfort.

Jaxon reaches across me and picks up the room phone. I hear the dial tone and then him pressing a button. Mama Sue's voice is loud enough that I can hear her through the phone and from downstairs.

"She alright?" her voice sounds thick with concern. I didn't mean to worry anyone.

"Better now. Bring up some of that soup? Lots of water as well," he orders, there's authority in his voice. Yet, Mama Sue doesn't question it, nor does she seem to mind it. He hangs up the phone, and there are questions lingering on my tongue, that I'm too afraid to ask. Jaxon seems comfortable, like this isn't strange at all. Perhaps this was what he wanted. Maybe he—

"You think even more than I do, Mira. After you eat, you can ramble off all your questions, and I'll answer every one of them."

I'm stilled in his arms. Did I say any of that out loud? No, I couldn't have.

"Did you drug me?" I question, half-jokingly, half serious.

He chuckles, and it brightens the room so much, I can almost see colors dancing against the walls. This is a nice change from all the arguing we've been doing. A pain shoots through my body, but I try my best not to react to it. I can feel a headache breaching the corners of my mind.

"Trust me, if I wanted to get you into bed, I wouldn't drug you and then cuddle you. You'd want me to be in your bed and inside of you."

He winks as he finishes his statement, and I swallow hard. I literally hear myself gulp in response. My head is craned in his face's direction, and his eyes. God, his beautiful blue eyes are boring into my soul. There's a lingering invitation in the quiet space between us. Jaxon's arms hoist me up; I'm so close to his lips I can taste the sweet aroma of his breath.

Jaxon's lips touch mine, and a chill rolls through me so cold, I feel like it's below freezing. My shoulders shiver, but not for long. Jaxon's hands caress the very hairs that are standing up on my cool, pale arms. The thick of his lips surround mine. He tucks and sucks, pulls and plays with my bottom lip, and I feel at ease. The pain subsides long enough for me to enjoy his soft mouth on mine.

Just as I submit to his hungry will, a knock comes on the other side of the door. He doesn't pull away immediately. Instead, his tongue penetrates my mouth and flails about, forcing my tongue to tango with his. It's easy to give in to him. Easier than I thought. His kiss is a temporary goodbye. Like a magnet, as he slowly pulls away, I rush forward toward him. He doesn't reject me; he offers more of his kiss. It deepens, and as he works his way to the edge of the bed, pulling me along with him, he places his hand on the back of my neck and gives me one simple command; "Wait."

There is no hesitation in him—no regret as far as I can see. I lean back on the pillows and watch him pull open the door. His shoulders are so large and husky I wonder what my legs will look like around them.

He turns around, his left eyebrow arched. I know he can't hear me, can he? My thoughts must be louder than I think.

"Oh, I'm so glad you're okay. Here, I made my special, family's soup. My grandmama made it for my mama, my mama made it for me, now I'm makin' it for you."

Caring as always, Mama Sue placed the bowl of soup that smelled of rosemary and garlic next to the bed and then placed the back of her palm against my head.

"Fever alright. Jaxon, run her a cold bath. That should help, right?" Mama Sue looks between me and Jaxon, and I can't say that I disagree, especially not with how aroused I am. I could use a little calming down.

"On it," he agrees and walks past the bed and into the bathroom. I attentively watch him as another pain shoots through me. It presses against my spine, and I'm convinced I must have the flu. My body begins aching, and my hands wrap around my center. If I squeeze hard enough, I won't come undone. A theology I've convinced myself of my entire life, and it rarely works.

"Rest, sweetheart. Do you want my help getting undressed?" Mama Sue asks. Normally, I would have been shy and said hell no, but I felt like my skin was going to slide off of my body at any moment. It seemed smart enough to say yes.

I nod my head, and Mama Sue gently helps me unclothe. I feel free, unalarmed. I know she's just trying to help me, but when I think about Jaxon being in the next room, I'm slow to wanting to get naked. If my pants come off, everyone in this room will scent my desire. I can smell it even through my jeans.

"On second thought, I think I can handle it. Thank you, Mama Sue." I politely smile, and she smirks. There's a spoken understanding between us, thankfully, and she rises to her feet.

"If you need anything..." She tilts her head, my head cranes in response. She twists her hips and heads toward the door, chuckling on her way out. My head shakes from side to side as she makes her exit. I manage to undress myself completely, minus my underwear and socks.

I'm doing my best to cover my full C-cup breasts, but my hands can't handle the spillage.

Jaxon appears in the door frame of the bathroom. His eyes advert my naked body, but he does not turn away.

"Let's try to break that fever," he says calmly, but his voice is laced with seduction, and yet another invitation, but this one I must ignore.

In seconds I'm on my feet, still holding my breasts, pressing my hands closely to my chest. I take a step toward the bathroom, but my legs feel like jello. I stop midstride to balance myself. My hands fall from my cupped breasts to steady myself against the bed post, but Jaxon clears the room in seconds.

His strong arms wrap around me and hold me up. I feel restless, and my body is aching once again. My skin feels like it's ripping underneath. I've never felt a pain this jarring in my life. I begin shaking as cold closes around me. My eyes roll to the back of my head, yet, I can still sense Jaxon close to me. Before my eyes completely close, a quick vision enters my mind, of a large, flaxen-haired wolf, bowing before me...

Chapter 12

JAXON

The fever can be a bitch, and it's not always a good sign. It does seem promising that she's in and out of consciousness, but with her body stirring up an unmeasurable heat, the cold bath I've put together for her should help break the fever and bring her back to consciousness.

There's no time for me to undress, and I won't place her, unconscious, in a tub full of water. Just moments before, she was in my arms, and I was caressing her soft skin. I felt strong with her near me, with her skin touching mine. But, as I'm holding her now, I fear losing her. I worry that she might not survive the shift that is inevitably coming.

My knees bend, and I cuff Mira's ass, lifting her into the air and closer in my embrace. After taking several paces toward the bathroom, I step out of my shoes. With her still in my arms I lift my feet, one at a time, stepping into the tub. Lowering us both in, I'm careful not to drop her in, and to slowly expose her as I let the water wash over the both of us. Now in the water, her arms are free, and I bear witness to her full beauty. The slight prickly raven hair on her arms and legs, I cannot ignore, and I hope that her wolf's mane will be just as beautiful and eye catching.

Mira doesn't wake immediately, but her skin is responding to the water with goosebumps. I know she'll wake soon, and the moment she does, we will need to speak of what she knows about her heritage and the truth of what is wrong. I can't stand another "flu" thought or comment.

Being this close to her, and with her in transition, I can hear her thoughts. At first, they were coming in whispers. I only thought I was hearing her. But her thoughts raced beside me.

Now in the water, I outstretch my hand, calling the water to me. I pull at my ancestral pack for strength and permission to wield the water as our pack has done so many times before. The water obeys my call and droplets of water crawl upon Mira's skin, dancing their way up her chin. The droplets kissing her cheeks.

My hand waves over her body, the water reaching each and every part of her. Her eyes open slowly, and just as she does, the water goes back into the tub. I no longer need it at my side.

"Thank you," I whisper, giving thanks to the water power that flows through my pack.

She looks at me, her cheeks reddening. I wash my hand over her face, unfazed by her embarrassment.

"We need to talk, Mira." I keep my voice steady. She is my mate, after all, and I don't want to scare her more than she probably already is.

"So soon? I still feel—"

"Sick, yes, I know, and you will until after your first shift. There are ways to bring it on," I suggest, fingering her arm with the back of my hand.

Her eyes are focused and trained on me, but she looks away, and her hands move to cover her beautiful breasts. Her flesh and gumdrop-like nipples become hidden from my sight.

"Shift? What are you talking about?" her voice quivers, and I can't tell if it's from the temperature of the water, fear, or sickness. I search her thoughts, yet I hear no fear. I feel none. Her eyes search mine for an answer.

"Mira, I believe you are a shifter, like me. A wolf shifter... and the way you respond to my magic, I believe you may be from my pack," I blurt out. It's better to just get it all out in one breath instead of going slowly. I felt like we'd been stalling too long as it is.

"A what? This doesn't make any sense, Jaxon. Maybe I'm hallucinating. The fever—" she starts, but I twist her around so that she's looking at me instead of lying in my arms.

"Mira, both of your parents have to have been wolves. That is the only way you'd be shifting now. That's why you're unwell. I know it sounds crazy, but there's no other explanation."

"Except, there is," she begins and rises from the water. Droplets fall down her body, swaying to the curves of her hips. She steps out of the tub, confidence and fresh annoyance flowing over her.

"Both of my parents are normal, everyday people. I think I'd know if they were wolves." Mira's mouth goes tight, and she turns away from me, heading back into her bedroom. I feel her frustration, her upset, and the unrest in her mind. She's questioning if I'm right, if I'm lying. If I'm crazy.

I rush to her side to clear the air, to detest the upset she feels.

"They might be, but if that's the truth, then they are not your parents, Mira. They may have raised you, but the truth—"

"Shut up, Jaxon! Just shut up, and why don't you get out! Gahhh every time we start to get along, you muck it up by pissing me off. JUST. GET. OUT! AHHHH!"

Mira places her hands against my chest and shoves me. It isn't enough to knock me down—it is enough, however, to make me stumble. I should have known then the pain she was going to experience. Her instant outburst was a clear sign that the change was at its peak.

The scream that ripped through her made me shriek in terror. The sound of her bones cracking and readjusting, the way her body contorts, she would tear up this room if I didn't do something and fast.

With a quick mind, I picked her up in my arms and took to the window. It wasn't open, and I could only hope that the glass breaking would be the worst pain she'd feel tonight, though I knew it would not be. The change itself is unpleasant.

"Jax-Jaxon, h-help me!" her screams come in panted breaths, and the window is my only choice.

Throwing us through the window, my only thought is how quickly I can get her into the woods before the change completely takes place.

I land on my feet, something I haven't done in ages from the height of that window and take off into the woods. As I run, her body convulses, and her bones break. Her spine snaps—I hear it, and then I see her hair begin to grow, but she's in so much pain, her body is struggling to complete the shift.

"Damn it!"

I place her on the grass blanketed ground, doing the only thing I can without interfering... wait for her to survive... or succumb.

Chapter 13

Mira

This pain is overtaking me. My body feels as though it's breaking and healing, and then breaking again. There's thick hair on my legs. I'm hairier than I've ever been in my life, and I can feel it as it grows in. My eyes shoot open, but Jaxon is nowhere to be found. I was just with him, and he thrusted us through a window, that we survived the fall too. He's either really strong, or I'm going really crazy.

I'm in the woods. The green shrubbery surrounding me is comforting, except it's not. It's pitch black out and the only light I can see is from the moon. As uncomfortable as I feel, there's something familiar about where I'm laying. Why am I on the ground?

My question is quickly answered when a large puddle of water begins sparkling. A small wave ripples through the center, and from the ground, it rises into one big water spout. I'm amazed, but I'm in so much pain, even moving a little hurts too much. Watching the water, I'm in awe when I see that the spout begins to mold into something, to form into its own special shape.

A wolf, I whisper. I notice its long snout and tail. Most of all, though, I notice its eyes. The wolf from my dreams. That's where I know this place. Though his fur is not amber, it's transparent, his shape is clear, and I know the smell of him.

I'm not afraid. Though, backing away isn't an option even if I was. The water wolf comes to me, his head is hung low. His snout brushes against me, and the coolness of his water fur splashes over me, soothing the aches and pains I feel.

My body shifts, and I lean into the water wolf, more. When he jumps up on two legs, I'm confused about his body movements, until he lands over me, in an embrace. His body is still transparent, and I can see through him, yet he feels solid as he lies over me. The pain subsides temporarily again, and I am grateful.

Then, I hear someone calling my name. Calling me to them. I turn away, just for a moment, and now Jaxon is there.

"There you are. I've got to find a way to keep you conscious. You won't survive if I don't," he whispers. His voice is trembling with concern. I'm not sure what's happening to me but becoming some sort of wolf doesn't seem right. Yet, as my body writhes in pain, shifting from left to right, as though the worst stabbing pain I could ever have is gripping hold to me. I can't help but wonder if he's telling the truth.

Jaxon's hand cups my face, and he brushes his knuckles across my cheek. If only my body could feel the way my heart does with him touching me.

Jaxon begins taking off his clothes. I would speak, perhaps protest, I'm not sure, but even thinking too much hurts. What happened to my water wolf? My mind is racing, and my heart is pounding. I can hear it in my ears.

Jaxon strips down to nothing but his skin, his glorious skin. His hair is loose and free. Several strands are in his face that I want to remove, but I can't move without causing myself more pain.

We're staring into one another's eyes. I trust this completely naked man, though we know very little about one another. One thing I'm certain of, is his protection feels real. His concern feels real.

Jaxon slides himself down to the forest floor with me. His body covers mine. His arms are aligned beside my head, and he's between my legs. If I didn't know any better, and if I felt better, I'd say something intimate was stirring between us. His warm body on top of me, though, feels... right. It feels good.

"I'll show you," he says, and then he leans down, planting a kiss on my lips. I can't kiss him back—my body is contorting about again; bones are tearing from my limbs. I shut my eyes; my body is in more pain than it has ever been.

But, with my eyes closed, I feel a weight over me, something much heavier than Jaxon's body. When I open my eyes, there's a large wolf on top of me. His face is beautifully menacing, yet I'm not afraid. His cream colored fur is tangled with strands of darkness. His hair reminds me of...

My thoughts shift, along with my body. My back arches from the ground, and a shrill cry comes from me.

I can't contain the pain I feel, and there's nothing I can do to stop what's happening. Jaxon, the wolf Jaxon, is licking me. His tongue is rough but welcome. As before, he's comforting me.

My legs extend, as well as my arms, and I feel my body being raised up from the ground. In seconds, the hair I'd seen before was no longer hair on my legs, but fur covering my body. My neck is outstretched, yet it isn't my neck that I feel. It too is covered with fur.

My feet and hands become paws that thud against the ground.

What the fuck? I attempt to say, and the words do come out, yet they don't come through my mouth.

I told you... I hear Jaxon's voice, but his mouth, his wolf mouth, does not move to say words. I try looking down at myself, and the only thing I can see are my paws. I circle around myself, trying to see what's become of me. There's a puddle nearby that calls to me, almost like a song.

I rush over to it and stare at my reflection. My raven hair is truly fur. My brown eyes are even browner, larger, and shielded by fur coated lids. My ears, no longer attached to the side of my head, are now pointed and on the top of my head.

Jaxon stares at me, and I can swear I see him smile. Do wolves smile?

Follow me, he instructs. He was right; I am a wolf, and so is he. There's more to learn, to find out, and I'd be a fool to not trust my own eyes. With more questions than answers, I have but one choice; follow Jaxon...

Chapter 14

JAXON

Running with Mira is exactly what I imagined being with my mate would be like. Learning and hearing her cadence is assuring and comforting. I could run like this with her forever. Watching her shift is the sexiest thing I've ever seen in my life. I've seen many shifters and helped several shifts, but Mira's shift was different. I fear losing my clan daily, especially from their first turn, but Mira, especially not knowing where she truly comes from, my heart sank knowing I might lose her to the very thing that is her birth rite.

Her dark fur mimics her hair. It's as black as midnight and she blends in with the night sky. But her deep brown eyes, they stand out amongst the darkness, just as the moon shines in the sky.

Mira keeps up with me as we approach my cabin from the back. She doesn't need to meet anyone yet; I'm thankful that we're alone and that no one is able to see us. It's late, and everyone except the guard is asleep. I hear their breaths, and I send them a telepathic message to stand down and keep away from the cabin. Tonight, Mira needs to rest. Tomorrow, we can figure out more about where my mate comes from.

On the cabin's back porch, I shift slowly, allowing my fur to disappear, and my four legs become two. I watch her, waiting for her to switch. I forget this is her first time; she doesn't know how to exactly. I drop to my knees, close my eyes, and place my head to Mira's.

Imagine your body. Feel the ground beneath you and think of how different your paws and your feet feel. Imagine your hands, your toes, your breasts...

I stop, realizing perhaps I've gone too far, but by the time I open my eyes, she's already changing. Her paws become toes, and her four legs disappear into two legs and two arms. Her wavy hair reappears, and instead of lying across the porch, she's standing on her two feet.

Her flighty eyes watch me, and then she turns around. She attempts to scan her own body, and it's clear she realizes she's not seeing what she just saw.

"Ja-Jaxon… h-how is this possible?" she questions and looks upon my face. I smile, remembering what my father told me as a boy.

"Many years ago, our ancestors were true wolves. They could not shift. This land belonged to them. They hunted here, made their own packs here, forging a life for themselves in the wild. Humans moved into the forest, stealing our resources, taking our food, killing us for our furs and selling our body parts for money.

It wasn't until a human… a witch, took pity on us, and she blessed the wolves. Though many see it as a curse. She allowed us to shift. We were no longer just wolves, but part human, so that we could learn to protect ourselves. As humans, we keep our families safe and protect one another. But our true nature, our true form, is that of a wolf."

Mira's pouty lips are open, and I capture them with my own. It catches her off guard, but she does not lean away. She leans toward me. I find her simply irresistible, and now that she's survived the shift, there's so much to catch up on.

I break our kiss and grab her hand, leading her into my cabin. It's been ages since anyone other than Pike has been in here, and I've never had a woman here. I would never dare. I've had my trysts in the past because waiting for your mate, or hoping for them, should I say, is hard. But, I've never been serious enough with anyone to bring them around my pack, or even allow them to be that close to me.

Mira is the first. And now, she will be my only.

There's a blanket on my couch that I use to cover her. I toss it lightly around her shoulders and pull the front of it closed around her body. Her cheeks heat up, abashed with redness.

"So... I'm really a shifter..." she utters, plopping onto the couch.

"You are, which means your parents are shifters. Your real parents," I reiterate. My mate's life is going to unravel, and I hate that she will have to experience this sort of trauma, but it isn't uncommon for shifters to be adopted, or at times given away for one reason or another.

I take a seat next to her and pull another blanket over the top of me, hiding my stiffened shaft that's growing as I near her.

Mate, my wolf encourages. But, I won't take her against her will. She still needs time to grasp all of this.

"I should have known, or at least suspected. I've been dreaming about a wolf for months. Same dream, every time. But this time, he was made... well, he was made of water," she clarifies, and I smile. This is a good sign, and she's more than likely a part of our pack.

"Tell me more," I urge her as I slip off the couch to find clothing for us both. Her voice rises as I make my way to my bedroom to select a few items for us, and she begins telling me of her dreams she had before, and what led up to her coming to the Appalachians.

Tonight, she dreamt of a water wolf, comforting her. That was no dream. She was truly experiencing that. I choose something easy for myself, athletic shorts and a t-shirt. I used to keep spare clothes in the living room, but I haven't shifted much lately, because I've been busy at Loch. It was nice to shift tonight for something other than danger or meetings.

I return to the living room with a t-shirt and a pair of boxers for her. She takes them and before the blanket drops, I turn my head. Even the thought of seeing her naked again has my wolf ready to burst out of my skin.

She slightly coughs, gaining my attention again, and now we're face to face.

"What you saw was most likely one of your ancestors, or our ancestors. A water wolf is a good sign. You had help tonight, during your shift."

"Yes, from you."

"No, from whoever your water wolf was. In the morning, we can go to the record keeper and find out more about you. It's clear there's a piece of your life missing, and she's the only person I know who can potentially help."

"Record keeper?" Her face reads confusion, but I intend to clear it up for her.

"Yes, but that's enough for tonight. You need rest. The first shift is the hardest," I mention, remembering my own first shift.

"I am a little sore, if I'm being honest. Do you have an extra pillow?" she asks as she takes a seat on the couch.

My heart stings that she'd think I'd let her sleep on my couch. She's a woman, my woman.

"I do have an extra pillow, on my bed, where you'll be sleeping," I explain and begin heading in the direction of my bedroom. When I realize she isn't following, I stand in the hallway waiting for her to join me. I hear nothing.

"I'm going to sleep in the other bedroom. My room is much comfier and already set up. It's not a request, Mira. Come to bed," I almost howl. From the swiftness of her movements, I know she knows I'm being serious. Not to mention her racing thoughts. Her growing arousal. I smirk. I'll have to tune her out if I'm going to get any rest.

Mira meets me in the hallway and together we walk into my bedroom. Her shoulders slump in relaxation, and I know now more than ever, she needs the rest she's afraid to try to get.

"If you need anything, don't hesitate to ask, Mira. You've been reborn in a sense and adjusting can be hard. I'm gonna check on you throughout the night to make sure you're okay. Don't panic if you hear me, but you're perfectly safe here. I wouldn't let anything happen to you—"

"I know, Jaxon. You've been very good to me. I'm... grateful," she speaks, and her arms come around me in a tight embrace. I take her in my arms and kiss the top of her forehead. It feels natural with her—nothing is forced, though neither of us are sure about our bond that's growing by the second.

When she releases me, I wait until she gets into the bed and settled before leaving my bedroom. I'm only a few feet away from my bedroom before I hear the words, "Jaxon, will you stay?"

I'm hesitant, but perhaps her wolf knows, though she hasn't made it known, that we are mates. Being away from one another too long will be painful, excruciating even, under the wrong circumstances.

"Of course," I consent, and climb in on the other side of the bed. This is going to be a very, very long night...

Chapter 15

Mira

I'm in the most comfortable position I could be. Jaxon's chest is warm but not hot. The few hairs he has aren't course, nor do they prick me. I always hated that in other men—their hair was tough and gross. Even after a night of shifting and running, Jaxon smelled like mother earth, not "outside."

"Quiet, little wolf, I can't shield your thoughts this early in the morning." Jaxon's voice is low and gruff. It sends a tingle riveting down my skin.

"You can hear me? Did you hear me back at Mama Sue's yesterday? Oh God, dear God," I gasp and throw the covers off me. This is mortifying. All the times I've thought about—

"Shh... you didn't know, and I'm working on shielding your mind from mine unless given permission, but yes. I can hear your thoughts and that of any wolf's. You will learn how to. I'm sure within a day's time, your mind will be overrun with thoughts. But, you have nothing to be ashamed of. And I'm certainly not disappointed in what I've heard," he explains, and my heart races. I wonder if he can hear it, it's so loud.

My palms sweat, as he stares at me, in what seems like anticipation. I don't know what to expect, but he comes to me. The distance between us does nothing to keep my mind or feelings at bay. He's on my side of the room, where I cowered, thankful that I'm not naked.

"Naked or not, I can see you, and I will not forget what I've seen... what I've felt," he reminds me of the small passionate moments we've stolen together.

Jaxon places his arms around me, something I've become accustomed to in just a day's time. Something I realize I look forward to. He eyes me seductively, and I welcome it, want it, even.

I can't hear his thoughts, yet, but I wish I knew what he was thinking, since he knows what's on my mind.

"I'll tell you anything, little wolf. I'm thinking about how your scent of arousal is rushing through my cabin and I went to sleep stiff. In the middle of the night, you found your way onto my chest, and rather than move, I pulled you closer. I'm thinking about how we've been fighting like wild wolves, and how it all makes sense now. You're feisty because you're yourself, but you're feisty because you're a shifter," he expresses and kisses my temple, dragging his tongue across to the other side of my forehead and planting another kiss on the other side.

"I'm thinking how I want to taste you. How I need to taste you." He trails kisses down my cheek, creating a river of intimacy between my cheek bone and now my neck.

My breath catches. I've never felt lips so soft and rough at the same time. My hands move in time with his kisses, rolling up and down the sides of his body. His lips touch my collarbone, and I exhale a heavy sigh.

Jaxon raises the hem of my shirt, reaching it over my head, and looks to me for permission. I nod my head, unable to do much else. I want this, too. With my breasts exposed, the morning air hits my pink gumdrops, bringing them to an erect posture.

Jaxon's mouth covers the left one, his right-hand kneading and squeezing the other. My head falls back in ecstasy, cushioned against the wall. He backs me up, and I squirm against him and the wall. His tongue flicking against me sends a sensation through me that I've never felt. My skin ripples, and I feel my wolf. She is the first thought I hear.

Mine, she whispers. I see her in the corner of my mind, rolling around on the ground, slowly, seductively. She wants this too.

"Calm down, little wolf, you'll shift."

His words are what I need to bring me back to him, though I wonder what she means by *mine.*

Jaxon, now on his knees, my breast still comfortably between his tongue and teeth. Walking his fingers down my stomach and flickers against the elastic of the underwear I'm wearing.

He pulls them down, and my morning dew is visible. Jaxon's fingers caress my folds, and I bite my lip. It's all I can do to keep from grinding against him. He growls as he nears me, and I hear my bones, I hear *her*, in my mind. She loves this attention, and we submit easily.

I place my hands in his thick and wild hair, pulling him closer to me. Jaxon's tongue begins to lap at my creases, finding my clit with ease. It's as if he's always known where to go. His hands firmly grip my backside, and I raise my leg, steadying it against his shoulder.

Jaxon's tongue is urgent, finding all the right spots. There's honey seeping out of me, and I cannot hold back what's been rumbling inside of me. My hips knock against his face, his tongue lashes against me, and I want more of it. He's sensing what I want, and he releases his firm hold on my ass.

He spreads my lower lips apart, partaking as much as he wants, and I want him to have more. His tongue eagerly takes me, rolling over me like waves in the sea. My wolf is pleased, and she's prancing in my mind's eye.

"You taste so good, little wolf," he says, and I can't hold back any longer. I release the breath I'm holding, panting wildly as I climax against his lips.

I pull Jaxon to his feet, meeting his lips with my own, until there's a knock on the front door. It jars us both, and we stop in our tracks.

"Jax, have you forgotten what today is?" a strong, male voice comes from the other side of the door.

Jaxon looks at me, and a smile fades as quickly as it appears. "Help yourself to a shower and anything in my closet. We'll retrieve your clothes a little later. We're going to see the record keeper soon," he explains and places a kiss to my lips. It's quick, but endearing. I'm just as confused this morning as I was last night, but with a little less pent-up frustration.

Jaxon leaves me to my shower, but I'm curious as to who's on the other side of the door. I go to the bathroom and start the shower. It's quaint and a walk-in, surrounded by finished wood. It's big enough for two people—hopefully Jaxon and I at some point.

The front door opens, and heavy feet enter Jaxon's cabin. I lean out of Jaxon's bedroom, attempting to hear the conversation, but I'm caught almost immediately.

"Shower, Mira. We have a long day ahead of us. The shower will soothe your bones."

I jump, his voice travels through the cabin and directly to me. So much for snooping.

***

When my shower is over, I enter his bedroom. I forgot to select clothing for myself, but there are a pair of jeans that seem fit for a woman, along with a t-shirt about my size. I wonder where they came from.

I dry my body and slip into the clothes laid out for me. Jaxon enters the room, and he is wearing different clothes than he had before.

"Where did you get these clothes?" I query, and he smirks.

"Afraid they belong to someone else?"

I forgot about him hearing my thoughts—that's exactly what I thought. I don't even try to deny it.

"They belong to a member of the pack. They can feel your presence here. They've offered help. That was Pike at the door this morning—my beta. He's going to look after Loch for me today, so that I can deal with... this," he gestures between us with his hand.

"And what exactly is this?" I retort, a question that has many meanings.

"One thing at a time, little wolf. We'll go see the record keeper, and then *this* we can discuss. There are boots for you in the living room. We can get some food after. I can hear your stomach from here," he chuckles, and his laugh is lighthearted. He seems much more relaxed than he was when I first arrived. I like this look on him.

What am I talking about? I convince myself to finish getting ready and slip into the boots in the living room. My feet squish around without socks, and I hold back the urge to say "Eww." The realization that I'm in the woods, in a cabin, with a man, a gorgeous man, surges through my mind. My life has changed so much overnight, and I suspect more changes are on the horizon.

With my boots on, Jaxon holds his hand out for me to take, and I do. When our hands join, a tickle surges through me, and I like the way he feels with me.

Jaxon opens the cabin door, and we walk through it. I'm able to see the pack members, the children, tiny wolves rolling around on the ground.

The way they separate, bowing their heads, in honor, it suddenly hits me. I replay Jaxon's former statement about his beta, Pike. That would make him the alpha. Jaxon snickers as we leave the pack and head deeper into the woods.

"What's so funny?" I ask as I almost stumble over several large branches. In theory it seems romantic to walk through the woods with a lover, if that's what we are, but in reality, it's difficult.

"That you've just figured out I'm the alpha, just another thing we need to discuss," he says as he helps to drag me along through the woods.

"Seems we've got a bit of time on our hands. Tell me about it now."

We stop abruptly, and my legs are finally given the chance to keep up with him. In step, we walk together, and he begins explaining, in detail to me, about the pack. How they're able to wield water, as many other packs are blessed with gifts of the elements.

Jaxon told me of his father's unfortunate death, and my heart aches for him. Though I knew him to be dead, I understand even more now the weight he's carrying, being a pack leader, owner of a dying business, and most importantly, a shifter in a world where he has to be kept a secret for his and his pack's safety.

We converse all the way to the record keeper's home, whose name I've been told is Celine. While I still have many questions, several have been answered, and I'm happy that some of this is starting to make sense, though my own story still has holes.

"Before we go in," Jaxon interjects, "she's a little... off, but she means well."

The words "off" and "well" don't seem to go in a sentence together, but I have no choice but to trust him. We approach a cabin near a creek, secluded and offset from the rest of the forest. We arrive at her door, which is simultaneously yanked open, and a woman, who looks as old as time itself, appears in the doorway.

"Alpha," she greets Jax first and then her eyes drift over to me.

"Celine. This is the human, who is not a human, I told you of. I was hoping—"

"I know what you were hoping. I felt her as she joined us last night. Come in, take a seat. Breakfast is almost ready."

"Then we won't keep you long," Jaxon says as we step through the threshold.

"No, you won't keep me. You'll join me. Already made enough for the two of you."

She nods towards us, and my face contorts with confusion. "How did she know we were coming?" I whisper, leaning into Jaxon.

"I know things you couldn't imagine, girl. Have a seat, I'll whip up your plate."

Celine, in ratty old clothes, takes to her kitchen, where the smell of bacon lures me in like a wolf... which I am. I guess that joke isn't funny anymore.

Celine returns with three plates, piled with food. Scrambled eggs, bacon, and toast, and for the first time ever, I know I'm not only going to finish my plate, but perhaps go for seconds.

She takes a seat across from us, near the lit fireplace, and picks up a pitcher from the floor. There are tin cups around it, and she fills each one with what I'm assuming is tea. When it touches my lips, I taste the sugar and know right away it's sweet tea—my favorite.

I lift a piece of bacon to my mouth and before I hear the "crunch," Celine looks over at me and says, "You've come for answers, and I'm going to give them to you. As record keeper, the water tells me things it simply does not tell others," she says, and snaps a piece of bacon between her teeth. She carries her plate with her across the room to a barrel of open water. Both Jaxon and I follow her to the other side of the room, our eyes trained on her and the water, our plates still in hand.

Celine places her plate down on the table next to her, and she rubs her hands together, as if she's warming up for something. She waves her hands over the water. I'm not sure what's taking place, but it's interesting for certain. The water rumbles, and a large sheet of water rises from the barrel.

Jaxon told me his pack could wield water, but I'm still surprised and shocked all the same.

In the water, there are shapes forming. The first I see is a wolf, my water wolf. There's a woman, slender but shapely, much like the shape of my own, standing over the wolf. The trees begin to form in the water, and instantly, I recognize this as my dream. The woman peers over the wolf. She strokes him lovingly. Until this moment, I'd always thought the woman in the dreams was me. I now realize it wasn't. That I must have been seeing someone else, someone I do not know.

The wolf violently shakes, water, that I'm sure is blood, seeps from him, and the woman throws herself over the top of him, tears rush from her eyes, and consequently, from my own as well.

As I continue watching, the woman shifts, and with her teeth she pulls the wolf until she no longer can, and uses her head to push him further to a cabin. She shifts back, but it seems to hurt her as she screams out what could be a battle cry, and she buries the wolf in the back yard of the cabin.

When she's finished, she enters the cabin and pulls up a floorboard where there is a small cry, no louder than a distant ambulance siren. Shortly after, a baby wrapped in a blanket appears. The woman strokes the head of the baby, kissing the top of its head and then places it in a basket, and then she flees the house with the basket, running toward the river.

Once she is at the river, the woman peels the covers back to expose the baby, looking over it and holding the basket closely to her heart. More tears breach her cheeks, and she kisses the baby once more. Then she wraps the baby back up, places the basket into the water, and sends it down the creek.

The sheet of water disperses, back into the barrel. With it, a breath of pain releases from me.

"I-I don't understand... I..." Jaxon's hands are on my shoulders, ever my comforter and protector.

"Our bodies are mostly made up of water," she starts. "Because of this, I can use the water inside of you, to paint a picture. To... call up your story. It seems you may be the child of myth," Celine says.

"Child of myth?" Jaxon and I both question. I'm wondering if it sounds as strange to him as it does to me.

"Yes. Your father did not have long before becoming alpha. Just a few years before, I believe. Your parents, Mira, were second in command at the time. He'd sent them on a mission, months before, to gather information on a neighboring pack that was moving closer into our lands. While we have been known to share our lands, we are entitled to know with whom we share them.

"Unfortunately, the other pack leader, Hank, did not see things this way, and he sought to take over the land, rather than share it. He became vengeful and spiteful of how his people enjoyed mingling with our pack, with our alpha, and he promised to get your father back for snooping. He could not kill an alpha without causing an uprising, so instead he killed your father to show his power. The wounded wolf.

Of course, this is all myth, but I believe this to be how you were orphaned."

Tears rush from my eyes. The life I have ever known is a lie. I can't deny the connection I feel to this story, nor that the beginning of this water wielded vision is the beginning of my dreams. My heart races, blood ringing in my ears.

My legs turn into jello, and I can almost taste the earth beneath me, until Jaxon's strong hold on me catches me.

"I'm okay!" I scream, with a voice that almost doesn't sound like my own. I'm hurt, my heart is broken. How is it possible to miss someone you never knew? My life, as I know it, has completely changed.

There's only one thing penetrating my mind. I need to leave. I have to get away from this place. My eyes shift from Jaxon, to Celine, and then the door. My legs answer my mind, and they carry me from Celine's, through the woods, with tears in my eyes, in the direction of Mama Sue's.

Chapter 16

JAXON

This door isn't thick enough to keep me from hearing her thoughts. I wish, with all my power, that I could fix this for her. That her hurt wouldn't be so painful that she felt the need to run away. But I understand it in a way.

I open her door and enter, to find her balled up in a corner on the floor. Her knees are to her chest, and her face is hovering over them. I can feel the water she's expelled pooled around her. She doesn't look up at me when I come in, but that doesn't stop me from going to her.

I toss an arm around her, pulling her in, hoping to lend her my strength. In my saddest and darkest moments, love from the ones who care for me most brought me through. Pike is one of the only reasons I can still walk around on two legs after losing my father.

If we were mated already, I wouldn't be able to fix the pain of this situation, but I would be able to ease her suffering a bit. The mating bond allows the other shifter to carry some of the weight, quite literally. The mating bond is probably what kept Mira's father alive for so long.

I'd heard of this child who'd been sent up the river, but I never gave it much thought. It seemed like... a fairytale, that there was a shifter shipped off into the regular world. It was never foreseen that the child would return, but I guess we all find our way back home somehow.

The mating bond was the answer, but she couldn't handle that right now. The way her disheveled hair hangs over her head, her reddened knuckles, I think she might have hit something. Which isn't odd—the fever probably awoke any dormant anger she had lingering inside of her.

Mira sniffles, finally acknowledging my presence. She looks over at me, and her eyes are so red and swollen. I hate that her heart is broken. I want to fix this for her.

My hand instinctively begins wiping away at her tears, but a fresh bed of new ones appears underneath these.

"I'm sorry. I don't know how to feel. I was never... different or special. I've always just been... Mira, and now all of these things are coming to light. I just don't know how to take it. I can barely get a promotion at work. Now I'm a shifter? This is insane," she says through a teary breakdown. Her shoulders are slouched over in defeat.

"You were always special. You just didn't know that THIS made you even more special. There's no doubt in my mind that even before this, you were something to be proud of, something to admire, Mira."

She kindly smiles, though it doesn't reach her eyes. I place my lips to her cheek, and an idea strikes me.

"Come on, I wanna take you somewhere."

She looks up at me with confused anticipation, but I think this might make her feel better, if she'll let me help her.

I hold out my hand, patiently waiting for her to take it. After a moment or so, she does, and I'm glad of it. She stands up, and as we pass the bed, in a teasing manner, she says, "What, no window this time?"

"Nope, but I can still carry you," I joke back, and lift her into my arms. She yelps as I hoist her into the crook of my elbows, and she wraps her arms around my neck, cozying up to me. It's clear, we both need this.

***

"It's beautiful," she whispers, and her eyes growing wide. I've brought her to the creek she's rumored to have been sent up, to the exact place. I recognized it from the water vision earlier.

"It is indeed. Listen," I take two steps toward her, and grab her hand, placing small kisses on the back of it. "I can't help you figure out everything, because some of your history is lost. I can, however, help you see just a little bit more. I wish my father would have told me more about this, then I would have a way to bring you solace, to maybe console you. But this is the only thing I can think of that might help... if you let me..."

Her eyes are tearing up, and she swipes at them like window shield wipers. Mira's chest rises and falls slowly. I'm afraid she'll say no, until she nods her head, and then agrees.

"Okay, place your hand in the water."

Her neck cranes like I've said something crazy and off the wall. With everything she's seen today, I would think a request so simple would be nothing to flinch about.

"Why?"

"Trust me…" It's a command, not a question. I'm her mate, and she is mine. She will eventually know there's nothing she can't trust me with. But, I don't want the mating bond to force her to trust me. I'd like to earn it from her. I have a feeling that when she finds out about the mating bond, she might feel as though her free will has been stripped. She's had enough adjustments today—she doesn't need another uncomfortable one.

Mira sticks her hand out and lowers it to the ground, along with her knees. She leans into the creek, her hand inching closer to the water. I follow her steps, and behind her, place my arms around her to steady her. A water vision can be powerful, but it can also be dangerous for those who don't know how to wield its magic.

Together, we place her hand into the water, and immediately it begins to swirl. The water jumps from its place and into the air, waiting to be wielded.

"What do I do?" she asks in wonderment, and I whisper gently, as to not frighten the awaiting water.

"Think about the vision you saw earlier. Think about your mother, your father, and let the rest do the work. Remember, the water holds our memories. We can use it. We belong to it, and it belongs to us. Visualize them in your mind's eye. Let your wolf help you."

Mira nods her head and closes her eyes. Her breathing steadies, and I know she's visualizing something. I try not to pry—something that's hard to do with her. I don't want to hear all of her thoughts, especially the ones she doesn't want me to hear.

When the water begins taking shape, she opens her eyes, and instinctively, her hand appears from the water. Mira opens her arms, as though she's giving the water a hug and the scene continues playing out in front of her.

Her mother leans over her, sending her with well wishes.

"I love you, Mira. Always and forever. I'm sorry things had to end this way, but at least you'll survive. This is the only way."

My eyes buck in bewilderment. I've never seen a water vision that had sound. There is a first time for everything, and this is truly the first time I've ever witnessed or experienced anything like this.

The water vision ends, and Mira's eyes are drawn to her hands, as though she's seeing them for the first time.

"I did it," her voice comes out almost as a whisper, but the smile on her face holds so much pride.

"Yes, you did. You're a part of the Loch Pack—water is our specialty," I remind her, and her smile hasn't dissipated. This is good news, but she looks tired, and she needs rest. Who knows when she might shift again involuntarily? She almost shifted earlier when I was feasting in between her thighs. We have to be careful until we mate.

"Right, I know, but I didn't expect that I'd be able to do it, though. Is that... common? For someone new to be able to have their first water vision, or whatever it's called?"

Her question comes with excitement. This is the happiest she's been in hours, and the pride she's showing in her ability gives me hope.

"It is common. It can still be difficult, but most are able to get it on the first try. The different packs have different elemental magic, so it's likely that most elemental shifters have a natural affinity for it."

"That's boring," she jokes, but there's a hint of disappointment in her voice, as though she wanted this to help set her apart.

"It is, but you did something I've never seen before. Your water vision had sound. That has absolutely NEVER happened before, at least not that I've seen. You're much more special than you think, Mira," I affirm, and kiss her cheek. My lips leave a heated spot of red that her fingers caress.

"Not even you? The alpha?"

"Not even me..."

Her shoulders inflate again, the first sign I've seen all day of her having hope, and I'm thankful for this moment, even if it doesn't last.

"Well, that makes me feel a teensy bit better," she giggles, and her face lights up. It's nice to see her smiling.

"Good... well, I guess I'll take you back to Mama Sue's. I'm gonna check in with Pike—"

"Wait, I was hoping I could go back to your cabin. I really don't think I need to be alone with my thoughts, or even myself right now. If that's too much to ask, I could—"

"Mira, you're more than welcome anywhere I am, at anytime," I assure her and place my hands on her shoulders, closing the space between us.

"I don't want to be a burden, I just feel like I unlocked this new piece of who I am, and I don't want to miss another second of it. You know?"

"And you won't. Come on…"

I hold out my hand for her to take it, and it seems this has become a common theme. I wait for her to take it, and each time, the timing between her taking it and me waiting for her to take it grows shorter and shorter.

Chapter 17

MIRA

"Now that you've been delivered back to safety, I'm going to check on Pike and get your things from Mama Sue's, if that's what you would like."

"Is that an invitation?" My eyebrows furrow in suspense. Since finding out about being a shifter and spending all this time with Jaxon, even though I feel confused, I feel something else. I've never felt before or haven't felt in a long time—safe. Jaxon makes me feel safe, and I love that he's answered any questions I've had thus far, which I have plenty.

One of my next questions will be to find out why there have been four wolves standing at the entrance of the pack lands since yesterday. I noticed them last night, and then again today. Maybe they just had everyday security details. I'd want to know soon enough.

"I told you before, you're more than welcome to be anywhere that I am. While I'm gone, feel free to make yourself comfortable. But I'll urge you to try and get some rest. Your body will need time to completely heal and prepare for your next shift. New wolves are unpredictable. It could happen at any time, and you don't want to be tired from the previous shift. That's how you get a wolf head and human body."

"WHAT?" I almost scream. My hands go to my mouth in terror.

"Just kidding, but seriously, take care of yourself. I'll be right back," he advises, and for the first time since our kiss, he walks out of the room and just leaves me. I'm not sure how to feel about this, but I don't want to make it more than what it is, yet, when he's gone I feel alone, like he can't return quick enough.

My life has changed so much in one day and I have feelings I didn't feel before, but this seems like a fresh start. New opportunities, and a chance to find out where I really come from. Though, I thought Nashville was where I really came from. I needed to have a conversation with Mom and Dad as soon as possible to confront them about the truth. Maybe they knew something about my birth parents, or at least my mom. I still need to work up the courage to ask them about any of it.

I cuddle up on the couch, allowing myself to get cozy. Jaxon's scent is all over his cabin, and he smells of sandalwood and bark. The perfect combination of man, musk, and sweet. There's a throw blanket hanging off the shoulder of the couch, and I'm tempted to grab it. More than tempted, because I do, and toss it over myself. In minutes, I surprise myself when I can't keep my eyes open.

And the next thing I know, I'm completely knocked out.

***

"I said rest, not wake the dead from snoring," Jaxon's boisterous voice wakes me. His vocal cords rub together and make something that sounds like music when he speaks. My eyes pop open, and I smell chicken and what I think might be waffles.

"How long was I out?" I wipe the sleep from my eyes, and rise from the couch, heading in the direction of the food I'm smelling.

"I'd say maybe an hour or so depending on how long it took you to fall asleep when I left here."

"Not long at all. Your couch might be a little too comfy," I admit. Back at home, my sectional couch was so comfortable all I had to do was look at it and fall asleep. I wouldn't have imagined I'd come out here to the forest and find something just as comforting, but I did.

My eyes and nose are led to the things Jaxon's bought into the house. He has all of my things from Mama Sue's, along with a bag of food from Loch Bar & Grill. Jaxon removes the food containers from the bag and sits them on the coffee table.

I was right. There was chicken and waffles, and the plate smells so good, I'm salivating just smelling it.

"Let me just go wash up," I call over my shoulder as I head to the bathroom. I hear a slight acknowledgment from Jaxon that he's heard me. I approach the sink, but there's a slight hesitation to stick my hands underneath the faucet. I'm a part of the Loch pack, so I should be able to wield water magic. I wonder if I can call water through the faucet without turning on the water.

I hesitantly place my hand under the faucet and close my eyes. I try to envision the water coming out of the spout, watering my hands. Yet, nothing happens.

A different technique, maybe.

I try again and think about the water lines that must be underground, I think about them flowing through the system of the town, and then it coming through the faucet, and again, nothing happens.

"What am I doing wrong?" I ask, as though the faucet or the water will respond.

"You need to have water, to call it. You have to be able to see it, to bring it forth. See?" Jaxon appears from behind me, nearly scaring me to death.

His muscular arms slide past my body and to the faucet, and he turns the knob just enough to allow the faucet to drip water. Jaxon sticks his hand underneath the faucet, and right away, water, as though the knob is completely turned on, comes rushing through the faucet splashing against his hands.

My mouth falls open, in shock, but also in frustration. Why didn't I think about that?

"You'll get it. Here, you try. And try holding your hand open. You have your hand in a crouched position.

Open it so that the water knows it's okay for it to enter," he instructs, and as he stands behind me, I feel strong and confident that I can wield the power he says I can.

For several minutes, we practice bringing forth more and more water until I get the hang of it.

"Come on, the food is getting cold," he mentions, and I follow him out of the bathroom.

Jaxon hands me my food and I'm about to take a seat on the couch, when he stops me with a look. His gaze is piercing, and his blue eyes shimmer as the sun is going down, but he looks at me lovingly. Jaxon slides underneath where I was going to sit and pulls me down into his lap.

"You can't eat if I'm in your lap," I giggle. His lips slip across the back of my arm, and he pulls me back closer to him.

"Of course, I can, but you just worry about yourself, for now."

My head agrees before I get a chance to say okay, and I settle into his chest, ready to erase the food on my plate, when I hear my wolf. It's a surreal experience to hear her, because it seems she is me, just a different version. I've spent some time with her in my dreams earlier, and we had a moment together, but I still have a lot to learn.

Mate, she whispers, and I instinctively say it aloud.

"Mate," the world playfully comes out, and Jaxon twists my body to look at me. The expression on his face says he knows what this means, whereas I don't know why my wolf would be saying this to me.

"Mate... what does she mean? Can you hear her?" I ramble, my questions come out quicker than I mean for them to.

"I can hear her; I can hear you. I hear you both..." he stops short of my other question.

"I know you can hear me, but why is she saying mate? Don't avoid my question, Jaxon."

My eyes focus on him as I wait for his answer. Jaxon fiddles underneath me, and he searches for the words to explain. My eyes are trained on him as I wait for him to speak.

"Your wolf is speaking to you, with the word mate, because-"

Just when we were getting somewhere, the front door to the cabin bursts, and Jaxon slides me off his lap, shielding me with his arm.

I look around him, but I'm not quite tall enough to see who's entered the room, but from the way Jaxon is standing in front of me, with his arm outstretched, this can't be good.

Chapter 18

JAXON

Camden burst through the door without knocking. The pack knows how I am about my privacy, and I'm sure news of my mate and me has spread. My scent has changed, or at least it should have because I've found her, and she's been with me. Our scents are now mixed. I haven't introduced her to anyone but Celine, and I don't want anyone to see her just yet.

But, with Camden busting in, I know something must be wrong. There's a reason for his impromptu entrance, and I'm determined to find out what it is.

"Camden, you know how I feel about my privacy. What do you want?" I grit my teeth, a growl lingering in my throat. Mira's hand is gripping my arm, urging me to calm down. I never imagined I'd be someone to be so protective over my mate, yet here I am, ready to tear Camden's throat out.

Mate her, you will calm down, my wolf encourages me, but mating her is not as easy as he may think. There's still so much to talk about, so many things to get her used to.

"I'm sorry, Jax, but Celine has been slaughtered. Her body was found in the woods just moments ago," he informs me, and I feel like someone just punched me in the gut. Behind me, Mira gasps, and I stumble backwards, almost falling on top of her.

"W-what happened? Who is responsible?"

I feel the glow in my eyes take effect. Who would want to hurt Celine? She did as she was told, and most importantly, she never sought to hurt anyone. She was a truth teller. Perhaps that's why someone would want to hurt her. Maybe she knew something that someone didn't want to get out.

I turn to look over at Mira, and her face is as red as a tomato with grief. I sit down on the couch and wrap her in my embrace. "It's okay. I'll find out what happened."

"We haven't, and there's no real evidence that I could see. I came straight to you and brought her body back home."

Camden's head hangs low, and I go to him. I clap him on the back, encouraging him. "Thank you for coming to tell me, Camden. Gather a party of men together. We need to investigate. I'm going to get in touch with Pike, and we'll all go together. Give me a second, and I'll join you."

I leave my instructions with Camden, and he nods before leaving the cabin.

"Jaxon, what does this mean? Why would someone hurt Celine? Is this about me? Is this my fault?" she asks, and my immediate reaction is to comfort her and make sure she knows that this isn't about her, even if it's related to her as a subject matter.

"No, baby, this isn't about you. Someone wanted to hurt us, make us weak. I need you to stay here so I can take care of this."

I step away from Mira and head to my room and into the back of my closet. My closet safe has been untouched for years, but if I'm to leave my mate in the house by herself, she needs to be protected. With her shift being new, I can't depend on her wolf to protect her, not yet.

The lock spins as I turn it and land each number perfectly to pop the door to the safe. When it opens, several

.9 mm with full clips are visible, and I take out two to give to Mira. If her shift fails her, she needs to be able to protect herself, though there's no doubt in my mind that the pack won't let anyone get this close to home.

"Do you know how to use a gun?" I search Mira's eyes for an answer, and she nods her head.

"Dad used to take me to the range. Jax, please tell me what's going on? I could go with you—"

"No!" I growl. "You can't. I can't lose you. You've had no formal training, no nothing. I promise, when I get back, I'll teach you everything I know, but right now, the pack is in danger, and I need to protect them. I need you to stay inside this cabin. No one, and I mean no one will get close enough, but if they do, blow their assholes off."

I hand her the two .9mm and she hesitantly takes them. I wrap one arm around her waist and pull her into me, kissing her as deeply as I can. "I promise, I'll be back."

My tongue twirls with her, a promise that I'll return to her. I haven't even made it official that she's mine yet, there's no way I won't be back for her.

Before leaving the cabin, I make a promise to myself, I won't let anything bad happen to her. I won't let this be the last time I see her.

Chapter 19

Mira

The clock on the wall ticks away. Several hours have gone by, and there's been nothing from Jax. My wolf is begging me to calm down, but she doesn't understand. I'm uneasy knowing that there's absolutely nothing I can do to help him.

If something was wrong, I promise you'd know it. You would feel it. He's our mate, she tells me, but that isn't comforting, because I don't even know what something like that means.

I've paced back and forth in the living room a thousand times, and no matter how much I walk, I can't seem to get myself to calm down. I'm falling for Jaxon, and the thought of losing him brings up all types of feelings I'm not necessarily ready to confront.

Trust me, he's okay... He's going to be okay, my wolf says again, and this time, her voice seems calmer. Perhaps we're okay together. Maybe I should lean on her for strength when I can't lean on Jaxon. I would have never thought I would, but he is my strength, my everything. I need him.

The couch is calling my name, begging me to sit on it, and I do. I calm down and take a seat, and when I do, the thoughts of my parents, birth and adopted, rush through my mind. I'm angry, and now being alone, this time has forced these thoughts to the front of my mind. I'm angry that they lied to me my whole life. I'm angry that my entire life, I tried harder, worked harder for a life that was never really mine to begin with.

Maybe everyone was right—I did have my life handed to me, and it was possibly because of me being adopted. I just happened to be the only one in the dark about it.

My phone is face up on the table, completely charged. There are many missed texts and calls from my mom and my boss, who I'm sure wants to ask me how things are going. I have no news on Loch, but plenty on me. None that he'll be interested in hearing, though.

I can at least call my mother—I know how she worries, and I hate myself for it. Regardless of the truth, she raised me and took care of me my whole life. The least I could do is call her back, and the least she can do is answer some questions.

I pick up my phone from the table and dial her number, reading the messages as I wait for her to answer.

"Sweetheart, I've been worried sick. Why haven't you been answering? Perhaps you've found yourself a mountain man to enjoy your time with, huh?" Her playful tone does nothing to ease the pain of my feelings. I'm conflicted on how to approach her and this situation. She's my mother, and I don't want to hurt her, even though I'm feeling hurt and lied to.

"Mom, I haven't called because I've been trying to muster up the courage to talk to you about something, and I just... didn't know how to bring it to your attention. Not to mention, there are a lot of new things happening in my life right now, and I'm trying to adjust," I speak honestly. I hear her inhale, and it's followed by her coined phrase.

"Sweetheart, you know you can tell me anything. I'll always be just an ear away," she says, reminding me of when I was a child, and she'd always preface her listening ear with this phrase, so that I would know I could trust her, that she would be there for me.

"I can tell you anything, yet that door doesn't seem to swing both ways, Mom. Why didn't you tell me I was adopted. I'm almost thirty! Don't you think I could have used that information before now?"

My heart beats wildly in my chest. I wondered what it would be like when I confronted her, when I told her I knew the truth, and none of the versions in my head came out friendly, or even like I wasn't mad, because if I'm being honest, I'm pissed off.

"Oh, Mira. Please try to understand, your father and I wanted to tell you. We just—"

"What? Didn't know how to tell me? I expect this from Dad. He's always been in and out, working odd hours, and he kept us fed, living comfortably, but you, Mom. You were always with me. Why would you hide this from me?"

"Mira, I'm sorry," she begins. "Please understand that I love you, and you are my daughter, I love you to death. Will you let me explain?" Mom pleads on the other end of the phone, and I feel horrible for upsetting her so badly. She's got tears in her throat, and I can hear her trying to clear them before she continues.

"You must understand sweetheart, when Dad and I found you, we were so happy. It was the best day of my life. I... I can't have children. I can get pregnant, but two or three months in, they always pass. Always. After six times, your father and I decided that it would not come to be."

"After we lost our last baby, we were on a trip. Your father would have done anything to make me feel better, and we were headed to the mountains. We ended up catching a flat tire on the car, and Dad had to change it. The weather was just turning from spring to fall, and the leaves were beautiful. I wanted to take a picture."

"We stepped out of the car together, and when we did, I began taking pictures, until I heard what sounded like a baby crying... you were crying. I rushed to the creek and found you in a basket with a blanket on top of you with your name stitched into it. You were a miracle, honey. Our little miracle."

Mom's sniffles crush me. I've questioned her about something I never knew anything about. I always wondered why I didn't have siblings, but I always thought they felt fulfilled with just having me. I had no clue Mom couldn't have children.

"Oh, Mom, I'm so sorry. If I had known—"

"How could you? I didn't tell you anything, and I should have told you sooner. I should have been more honest, more forthright, but I wasn't. I'm truly sorry. Dad and I promised we would tell you at some point, but as the years went on, it just never happened. Please tell me you forgive me? That this won't be the end of our relationship."

"Mom, of course not! I'm hurt, yes. But, I will heal. I just want to know if you know anything about my birth parents. If you have pictures of them by chance?"

"I actually do, sweetheart. When you were about four, I had a DNA test run on you. Turns out, your mother and father have a past, and we were able to figure out who your family was. We never found out if there were any grandparents. Give me a few hours and I'll find the photos. I'll send them over to you—"

Mom is midsentence when the door to the cabin swings open. He looks filthy, tired, and the serious look on his face tells me that there's a pressing issue, maybe even worse than Celine's death.

"Mom, you do that. I have to go," I hurriedly say and hang up the phone. I'm on my feet in seconds, and Jaxon pulls me into a kiss. My lips hold to his for seconds before he lets go and says, "We need to talk…"

Chapter 20

JAXON

The sight I saw was gruesome. Since becoming an alpha, it's been harder than ever to manage the pack. I grab Mira's hand and take her to the back of the cabin. I lead her to the bedroom and take a seat on the bed. I gently pull her into my lap, settling down into a comfortable resting spot.

"Before Celine was murdered, and we played the scene out in her barrel, she left us a message in her record book. Hank, the former alpha of the Tinct pack, will not stop until the missing child dies. But I'm going to kill him. I won't let anything happen to you, Mira. That's my promise to you. Anyone who wants to hurt you will have to go directly through me."

My voice turns cold, but my hands find warmth around Mira's waist. With her in my lap, I feel stronger than I've ever felt. I can share my burden with her, but also reassure her that she's safe with me.

"Jaxon, is there another way? Why would he want me dead? Why would he want blood? This has to be about more than just someone snooping..."

She's right, and I know there's more to the story, but I've yet to discover it. Pike arrived late, but that was better than not at all. He would have had the situation completely assessed before we ever even approached. I cant take back what occurred, but I can help set it right; for Celine and for Mira.

"You're right, and I'll figure out what this means, but first, I must take this to the pack. I need to see what they have to say. This could bring a war to our doorstep, and I need to make sure our people are ready," I explain. She twists in my lap, looking over her shoulder and into my eyes. I hear her wolf calling to me, and mine to her. We need to mate, but I fear what will happen if we do and I die. Then she'll never be okay. I will have brought her into this life, changed her own, and ruined everything she knows for almost nothing.

Yet, the urge is still there, and I can no longer deny it.

"Jaxon, tell me, why does she keep saying mate. You were going to tell me earlier... tell me now."

Mira places her hands on either side of my face. She looks to me for an answer that she desperately needs, and I want to give it to her. I have to. I can't take her against her will, without her truly knowing what it is she's asking for or getting into.

"You're my mate, and I am yours. We are destined to be together. Wolves mate once; they mate for life. You are directly tied to me, and I'm directly tied to you forever. Once mated, everything you feel, I will feel. Everything that happens to me, it will be like you have a first class seat to experiencing it. Our bond, though, will make us inseparable. We'll never be able to be parted, nor will you want to be. In the event that I fall, you will more than likely feel like you're dying, like you're off balance forever. Losing a mate is worse than death itself..."

There are pros and cons to mating, and the biggest con is knowing that you won't be with the person completely destined for you ever again. It hurts more than a mortal wound.

"That sounds awful... how does the mating bond occur? How do you... solidify the bond?" she asks me, and I could answer right away, but I'm shocked that she's taking this so well.

"You don't have any doubt that I'm telling you the truth? You believe me when I say that we're mates? That we were destined for one another?"

"I do. My wolf has been trying to convince me all day. I can feel what she feels, and she feels what I feel. I'd be lying to say that we don't have a deeper connection than I'm used to. How do we seal it?" she asks again, and rather than saying it, I meet her lips with my own, pulling her neck closer to me.

Her body responds immediately, turning around in my lap. Her legs are now wrapped around me, and her arms are snaked behind my neck.

"This... this is how we mate," I whisper, and Mira smiles with understanding. Gently, I push her wavy hair from her face and lift her from my lap, spinning her around and laying her on the bed, with her back to it.

I'm in between her legs, and I can smell her arousal permeating the room, staining the very jeans she has on, but I love her scent, and it's driving my wolf mad. He's rushing to the edges of my mind, begging to be let loose, and I'm going to set him free when I find my release.

Mira stares at me with anticipating gazes as she glides her tongue across her bottom lip, enticing me. I lick her lip where her tongue brushed it. Mira's back arches as she meets my lips once more.

My cock stiffens, pleading to be let out of its clothed cage. Mira spreads her legs wider and allows me in deeper between them. I bare my teeth and begin to pull at her pants, unbuttoning them swiftly.

Mira assists me, wiggling out of her pants. Her shaven center flashes me in the face, and I can't wait to taste her again. Mira's glistening folds invite me in, and I won't ignore them or deny her satisfaction. I sink my lips into her centerfold, and she releases a moan so loud, I'm sure the entire pack hears it.

"JAXON!" she screams as I take her over the edge with my tongue. I flick her clit back and forth with a steady rhythm, and she grinds toward my face.

"You're gorgeous," I murmur against her gorgeous pussy. The way her body shakes and writhes in ecstasy sends chills down my spine and straight to the tip of my dick.

She giggles, and it's the sexiest thing I've ever heard. From between her legs, I can see side tresses of her beautiful, darkened hair, hanging off of the pillow.

"Please, Jaxon, I-I need you inside me," she moans, and I want nothing more than to give her what she's asking for.

Quickly, I remove my jeans and climb back onto the bed. My shaft is at full attention, ready to invade her mating space.

"Once I claim you, you're mine forever. Understand?" I question her again. She nods her head with vigor, and I guide myself to her. I rub the tip against her clit and tease her entrance. Her face twitches, and her mouth hangs open as she watches me.

When I slowly push and enter her, her eyes glow the most beautiful dark brown I could see, and her head thrusts back against the pillow. Her eyes close as she allows me to take her. She's so tight and wet, I could release in her now.

Our bodies grind together, thrusting in the same melodious rhythm. She wants this just as much as I do, and I couldn't have imagined our mating going any better.

Mira scoots closer to me and cranes her back off the bed, rolling her hips against me, as I thrust forward into her.

"You feel like heaven," she whispers, and I lose myself in her.

Ours, my wolf says.

Ours, hers responds, and I feel our releases about to cum.

Mira's nails dig into my neck, and I accept her mark. I hope the cuts go deep enough to mark her territory.

My dick twitches, and I hold onto her. This is the hardest I've ever come in my life, and when I reach my climax, she reaches hers. She contorts on my cock, sucking me in even deeper and emptying all that I've got. It's all for her.

"I love you, Jaxon," she moans as I watch her come down from her climax.

"I love you, too, Mira," I concede, and I feel my eyes glow ocean blue. Our mating bond is complete. Mira's arms are still wrapped around me, and I never want to let her go, but the pack needs me, and there are more pressing matters at hand. But for now, I'm holding onto her, and we can enjoy this moment, before our lives return to being in ultimate danger.

Chapter 21

MIRA

If I had known mating would feel like that, I would have done that a long time ago. All I've ever wanted was to feel the way I felt with Jaxon, with anyone else. But I know now I couldn't because Jaxon is my mate, and he was waiting for me. I just didn't know he existed.

Jaxon gathered the pack and asked them to stand with him during the fight he would eventually take to Hank. I was shocked to see that the pack was willing to come together for a cause that had nothing to do with them.

But, it was unanimous. There were many elder members who remembered my parents, who wanted to help avenge them. I couldn't believe that, but to hear that, it let me know they must have been good people.

My mom sent me a photo of my parents. I took after my mom in most ways, especially in her shape, but I had my father's eyes and eyelashes. They were a beautiful couple, and I wish I could have met them in my adult life, just once.

Over the last few days, I've been trained in combat to defend myself and anyone else who might need it. I'm not great at wielding my water magic, but Jaxon and I are growing closer through our training, so that's a plus.

My body has been beat up. My wolf has been yanked around, up and down, and the only positive about this is I've been able to control my shifts. I've learned how to make my shifts go faster, and it's become much less painful. I'm fortunate to have at least mastered that, and whatever I can't handle as a wolf, I can shoot as a human.

Everyone has been especially helpful, including Pike. We haven't had as much interaction, but the few times we've been around one another, he's been kind, doesn't doubt my abilities, and we've become fast friends, along with several other members in the pack.

"Take a break little wolf. You need to rest your bones. I think that's enough for the day," Jax calls out to me, sweat dripping down his chest. He looks so sexy; I can't help but run my tongue across my lip. I want to taste him outside, but he's been working with the pack long hours to get them ready for anything that might happen.

The security details at the corners of the pack lands switch out every four hours. Jaxon has been making sure they each eat, get rest, and that they're okay the next time their shift starts. Jaxon is such a good leader, and it's obvious that his father trusted him to take over. If only he had left him with some financial security—that would have been even better.

But now that I know how the pack lives, I understand why the business is struggling. Many of the pack members have side hustles and gig jobs, but no real work to pay for expenses the bar incurs. But, one thing at a time. There's already a lot on our plates. Our... plates. I like the way that sounds.

When I enter the cabin, I find my phone ringing. I'm soaked in sweat, and my jogging pants and t-shirt are literally sticking to me. But I can't ignore the call from my boss. It's been six days. My last day would be tomorrow, and I can't ignore him another second. He's been calling incessantly. It's time for me to face the music.

I pick up my phone, and Mr. Sanderson's voice is anything but pleasant.

"Mira, why haven't I heard from you?"

"Sir, I've been meaning to call you. All is well, and we are on track," I lie. It's the only thing I know to do. I haven't exactly figured out how my life will be going after this. I know for a fact that I won't be without Jaxon. Now that we're mated, when we're even a few miles away from one another, at times, I feel a tug in his direction. He feels a tug in mine.

But staying in the mountains wasn't supposed to be a part of the plan. Losing my job and the promotion that could potentially come with it wasn't supposed to happen either.

"I see. I'll be expecting your paperwork in the next couple of days?" There's a hanging question behind his statement, and I "mhm" him, leading him to end the call.

As I put my phone back down on the table, I smell my mate behind me. His scent is even stronger to me now than it was before when I could simply smell his breath or what I believed to be his cologne.

"So, what are you going to do?" Jaxon takes a seat across from me in his green and blue plaid recliner chair and takes off his boots. His eyes are weary with thoughts of war, but he's doing his best to shield it.

"Do about?"

"Your job. Your life. What are you going to do?"

It isn't like I didn't know we'd have to have this conversation. I'd just hoped that it wouldn't come so soon. But, my business trip would have been over tomorrow anyway, and I would have been returning home, but Jax and this pack are my life now. Everything has changed. Leaving them feels... wrong. As afraid as I am to stay, I'm more afraid to leave, of what will come of my life if I go home.

"Jaxon, I can't leave you. Surely you know this. I'll give it a few days, and then I'll just quit. Real estate is everywhere, you know?" I shrug my shoulders, and he reaches for me. Like a magnet, I'm drawn to his dreamy, stargazing eyes, and take his hand. He pulls me down into his lap—my favorite place to be, and he rubs his hand over my cheek, intently watching me.

"I don't want you to quit. Somehow, we can make it work. I can come visit—"

"Shh... I don't want you to come visit, and I don't want to visit you. I've seen the way the others in the pack live with their mates. When I'm with you, I feel whole, and I don't want to lose that. Maybe this is the push I need to start my own business. I've got the money saved up. Maybe we can use some of the money to save Loch—"

"Mira, as much as I appreciate what you think you're about to offer me, I can't let you do that. Loch Bar & Grill is my responsibility, not yours."

I'm stunned by his reaction and the venom in his voice. He doesn't seem thrilled with my words, but as his mate, I feel I should be able to offer him help, and he accept it.

"And as much as I appreciate your response, you can't tell me what to do with my money, and you need the help. I can be of help if you'll let me be," I whisper the last part and kiss him. Normally, I let him take the lead, but this time, I think he needs to see the power that I possess.

I pull at his shirt, ripping it down the center. Being around the wolves has made me stronger, even in my human form. Jaxon stands up, and I stumble to my feet but quickly recover. I slip out of my sweatpants and take off my shirt. He follows my lead and does the same. Jaxon's scent is even stronger when he's naked, and it calls to me like our magic does to water.

Forcefully, I knock him back into the chair and I climb on top of him. I'm already wet from kissing him and just being near him. I want Jaxon in me as much as his body will allow.

I lower myself onto his thick and hard shaft, taking him inside of me slowly. Jaxon's hands grip my hips as I ease my way onto him, and I shift my hips around in a circle. He tries to gain control by thrusting upward, but I shake my head and begin bouncing on his stiff cock.

"You'll let me help you, just like you'll let me make you come, won't you?" I look him directly in his eyes, and we're connected. He's strong and wants to resist me, but the tighter he grips my hips, the more I know he can't tell me no and truly mean it.

"You're going to be the death of me, woman," he grunts, and I laugh.

"I'll go to death with you," I whisper and ride him into oblivion.

Jaxon's mouth settles on my right nipple, and the pleasure shooting through me courses through me like blood.

"Yes!" I scream. Between his teeth, I feel him take my nipple. He nibbles on it, and I feel my climax is near.

"Whatever you want," Jaxon whispers, and I bounce on him some more. Our skin slapping echoes off the cabin's walls.

"Say. It. Again!"

"Whatever you want, Mira. Whatever you want, forever," and with his admission of "forever," I come undone. Jaxon follows me into our loving bliss, and rather than move, I stay on his lap, and shortly after, I find a peaceful sleep.

Chapter 22

Jaxon

After an unexpected nap, and a shower that led to more lovemaking, I've convinced Mira to speak with some of the pack to ask questions about her parents. We found out their names were Jillian and Myron, for which Mira; she was named after her father.

"What if they don't want me to ask?" she gripes, leaning onto my side.

"How anyone could refuse you, I don't know. You've singlehandedly won over the hearts of everyone here. Just today, I heard someone mention how you bring light to the pack. I feel it, and I know others do as well. They are your family—no one will turn you away," I correct, hoping that my answer has provided her with some solace.

"Okay, okay, no need to lay it on so thick. I'll go mingle," she agrees, and I'm thankful. When I see her speaking with Armena, Cordelia, Sanya, and Karah, I know that she'll be occupied for a while. This gives me the opportunity I need, unfortunately, to sneak away.

Pike is waiting for me just outside of the camp, and while she's busy talking, I sneak off, headed to meet Pike. I just hope she will forgive me for what I'm going to do. As the days have passed, it's become clear to me that taking care of Mira must be my main priority. Though she was born a wolf, she does not know how to completely be a wolf. She wasn't raised here, and while she's progressing in her training, she's not nearly fast enough, strong enough, nor strategic enough to defeat an enemy like Hank.

I have to kill him tonight, before he's able to strike us.

"You sure this'll work? She's a smart woman; she'll figure it out," Pike points out, and I know he's right, but by the time she figures it out, I'm hoping that Hank will be dead.

"Only one way to find out," I retort and look on at Mira from a distance. I can only hope that I make it back home to her, and if I do, we can put all of this behind us and move on with our lives. Hopefully, I'll have the opportunity to be with my mate until our ancestors call us both home.

Before taking off with Pike, I scan the forest, and there are several of our strongest pack members waiting for us. I turn to join them, but not before stealing another glance at my mate, who I can only pray I make it back to.

Chapter 23

Mira

"Your mother was gorgeous! The kind of woman who could stop another woman's breath because she was so gorgeous. Wasn't she, Cordie?" Sanya directs her question at Cordelia, who nods her head with a smile. She seems very polite, but a bit distracted.

"And your father? What a hunk! I'm not surprised you landed the alpha. If Jaxon's father hadn't been alpha, your father would have been an amazing second choice. A real leader he was," Karah adds, and my heart thuds with pride.

"Sounds like I come from good stock."

"The best," Cordelia interjects, and I'm happy to hear this. I've been sitting here with these women for the last hour. They've told me every story they could possibly remember about my parents, Jaxon, and about the pack.

It isn't until I see the night sky completely darkened that I notice Jax has completely disappeared. Not just him, but several others who are typically out and about during the night's campfire. My head is on a swivel as I look for the others, but I see very few faces I've seen over the last few nights.

I've been working on my telepathic bond and trying to strengthen communication. I close myself as the women around me continue to talk. The fire burns brightly around us, yet it's dark enough that the shadows of the night shield my face. No one can see how hard my pale face is concentrating.

Where are you? Why'd you leave?

Please forgive me...

Jaxon, what's going on? Where are you?

I search my mind for a response, and when none comes, I know I need to go and find him. He thinks I'm a fool, and perhaps I let him believe that I am. Panic sets in. Why would he just leave and not tell me? I knew he was under more pressure than he was letting on, but when I said he was, he tried to make me think I was crazy.

There was no time to alert anyone. Everyone was in such a good mood, and I knew he had tricked me on purpose.

Help me, I call out to my wolf, and she's there, ready to help me find our mate. She nods her beautiful head and leads me toward the edge of the pack land. I have to be stealthy, so the guards don't see me. It's overwhelming, and I haven't had the proper training, but where Jaxon is concerned, I'm too attached now. I can't... I won't lose him.

I hide behind one of the larger trees that resembles a Christmas tree. The branches hide me and keep me out of sight, just long enough for me to distract the guards. When it proves they aren't going to move from their post, I have to make them. I do the only thing I know to do and grab several rocks and throw them in another direction, catching their attention immediately. They hear the whizz fly past them, though my rocks don't land nearly as well as I've planned for them to.

But, it's enough to get them out of the way. When they step away to check out what they've heard, I run in the direction my wolf tells me to. I don't stop. She sees a trail I simply do not. She's much better at hunting than

I am. In my mind, she's highlighted a trail for me, based on the footprints on the ground.

He's shifted. He's on all fours, she guides me, and I thank her. I see what Jaxon meant now when he said we are one, though we think, at times, separately. She's almost like my conscious, my second brain.

Use the water to shield yourself. Trust your power, trust your strength, she instructs, and I'm afraid. I want to remain unseen in the forest, but I have no idea how water can help do that.

"But how? Water is transparent—I will be seen."

But, water can also be used as a cover, to cover your sound, so no one will hear you. There's a creek just to your right.

She's right, there is a creek. Jaxon says all you have to be able to do is see it, and you can call it to you. I take a deep breath, and do as I've been instructed to do, hoping that this time, when it comes down to my mate's life, that this time, my wield will be perfect.

I open my hands, palms down, the way Jaxon insists, to let the water know it's okay to come to me. I watch the creek, summoning it with my heart, instead of my mind.

I need this to work. I don't have the same skillset that the other wolves have—I must be strategic and smart.

Help me, please, I almost beg it, yet I do not have to do so. I feel the tie between myself and the creek. Jaxon told me he'd never seen someone control sound with their water vision; I could only hope I'd be able to control it and make it louder.

The water comes to me, crawling across the grass, covering my feet, but I don't feel wet at all. It wraps its way around my legs and then comes to my hands. I have a never-ending source if I just keep walking.

Amplify, I ask of it, and the rushing noise of the creek grows louder. I continue to follow the trail, and as I get closer, I become nervous, afraid even for Jaxon, and I hear the water begin to calm down.

No, please don't abandon me, I plead, and almost instantly, the water begins rushing above its sound level again. If we survive this, I can't wait to tell Jaxon about this. I'm determined that our story will not end the way it did for my parents. We've only just met—I can't lose him so soon.

I've been walking for what seems like hours, and when I've neared my mate, I can not only feel him, but I can smell him. His blood, sweat. I can sense his frustration, his worry.

My bones begin to ripple underneath my skin, and my wolf wants to come out. She's my only real protection, so it makes sense to release her. Since shifting isn't so hard anymore, I let her out, and she comes at will. My legs become four, my hair, dark as the night rushes over my skin and becomes my fur, and I'm hunched over now, completing the transformation and releasing the water.

Following Jaxon's scent, I find him, bloody and tied up. Several of the pack members are dead, yet Pike remains. It's a horrific site. All the blood. The severed body parts. I've grown attached to these people—my people. But, seeing Jaxon and Pike alive brings some relief.

Jaxon notices me right away. His eyes go wide, and he's not happy to see me. He's in his human form, in which he's still strong, but he could maul his enemy as a wolfperk of being the alpha.

"Mira, leave." His voice is gruff with frustration and anger because of my presence.

I will, just as soon as I have you and Pike. I gently rub my snout against his stomach, where there are several slash marks. I become angry at the thought that someone hurt my mate to this degree, but we don't have time to talk about what happened.

With my sharpened fangs, I bite loose his ties, and he exhales a heavy sigh when his arms aren't tied behind the back of the tree.

"Run away, Mira. Please, save yourself. I'm hurt, but you can get away," he pleads. He should know by now; I will not leave his side.

Not until we're all gone, I remind him, and he shakes me off, sliding to the side of him and untying Pike as well. He has a similar reaction to being cut loose.

Can you shift? I know we'll get out of here much faster if we're on four legs than two.

"No, not right now anyway. We need to get to the water. I can heal some if we get close enough to it," Jaxon informs me, and even in his weakened state, he's still trying to support Pike, who is beaten up terribly. Jaxon allows Pike to lean on him, neither of them able to shift.

Both of you, on my back. We'll head back to the pack lands, and we'll recoup, and it's not a request. Get on me, I growl. This isn't the time to be going back and forth, with egos flaring.

"I told you I liked your mate," Pike speaks, a chuckle coming from him.

"And I told you, I'd kill you if you said that again, come on," Jaxon retorts with sarcasm, and the two of them mount me, but not with ease. They're so sore and in so much pain, their wounds are graver than I had feared.

With them finally on my back, I turn around and head towards home. I've made it just past the first set of trees, and I can taste our freedom when I hear branches snapping to my right. I've seen enough horror movies to know not to follow the branches.

Instead, I veer to the left, where there is more snapping. I can only run straight ahead, and when I do, I run smack dab into another wolf, just stopping short of him.

I'm surrounded, even behind me, by four wolves. Just when I thought we were going to survive this, another challenge presents itself.

Chapter 24

Jaxon

Attacking Hank head-on had not been the victory I hoped to achieve. He was ready for us, almost. It seemed like he'd been prepared, but when you've been plotting revenge for two decades, I guess you would be ready for anything that might occur.

Our wounds wouldn't have been so bad if we hadn't been fighting to save everyone, and we lost them anyway. My pack members sacrificed themselves to save Pike and I, only for us to be captured in the midst of it. I wanted to keep Mira away from danger, and instead, she runs to it, as though she's a warrior. I've made it plain to her; she isn't the best fighter, but that doesn't mean she doesn't have skills.

But not enough to face Hank. I suppose if I'm going to die, the best way to do so is by protecting my mate. I won't be able to live with myself if she dies and I survive. Tonight, we either go together, or I go alone.

I'm unable to currently shift, but with four snarling wolves on our tail, I'll have to fight them. I'm still strong, just not as strong. I hop off Mira's back and twist to look at Pike. His sentiments are the same as mine, and we are both on the ground, ready for an attack.

"Please listen to me, and run, Mira. Run back to the pack. They can protect you."

And who's going to protect you and Pike? Neither of you are in any condition to fight.

I don't get the opportunity to respond. Mira jumps to her left and attacks the first wolf, who's about her size. He's small and puny for a male wolf, but Mira doesn't look puny—she looks like a warrior now, the way she immediately goes to take out his jugular.

The wolf to the right and from behind attacks Pike and me. I wrestle my wolf to the ground, shockingly easy, and I snap his neck, just in time for the other wolf to jump in on the action.

The wolf bites at me, and I know it will only take one bite from him to end it all. His jaw is as powerful as a shark's. I love my own fangs, and I'm not afraid to bite down on anything, so I know this wolf won't hesitate. I throw a punch, and Pike and I are now back to back. To my right, I see Mira, she's handling her own, for now, but my goal is to get to her.

But this wolf is clever, he goes to try and take my legs from underneath me. All he needs is to get me to the ground, and he's won this fight. I jump around, hoping to tire him out. Wolves are fast, but moving a lot, especially in circles, is overwhelming for our bodies.

Pike is able to subdue his wolf by stabbing it in the top of its head with a tree branch, and just as the fight is almost over, I feel a presence approaching us. It's Hank.

Rage grows in me. He's a coward who has let others fight his battles, but he of course, approaches Mira. Hank has fully shifted, and he's large, even larger than I am in a full shift.

"I'll handle him," Pike refers to the other wolf I've been wrestling with so that I can focus on Mira.

It only takes a second for me to turn around, but in that second, Hank has head-butted Mira against a tree.

"NO!" I cry out, seeing my mate crash into the center of the tree. She's hit it so hard that bark comes off.

Though I could not shift before, seeing my mate in this state has brought my wolf out. In seconds, I'm on all fours, and I'm rushing toward Hank. I hear Pike over my shoulder yell, but when I hear the snapping bones of the other wolf, I know Pike is victorious.

I charge Hank, but he glides out of the way. He's light on his feet even with his stature. I reposition myself, to stand in front of Mira. I will die to protect her if I must. My snout is low to the ground, my teeth are fully exposed and ready.

You're a fool, you know? You've brought me exactly what I want, Hank starts. Even his voice sounds evil.

Leave her alone, fight me. Let's end this.

End this? Oh no, she will pay for what her parents started. You see, after Jillian sent her up the creek, she came and sought revenge for me killing her mate. She didn't come right away. No, she watched and waited for me to leave. I had... other business with the bear shifters.

While I was away, she slaughtered my entire family, and now, I have no heir and hardly any pack. She killed my mate, and my children, and now there will never be another alpha directly from my lineage.

Fair is fair. When I found out she killed my family, I hunted her to the ends of the earth. She left the Loch pack, and I found her hiding in a nearby city. She thought she could hide from me—but she couldn't. When I crushed her bones with my own teeth, I thought this was it. I didn't know anything of her baby. It was later rumored by spies from other packs that she'd given birth to a daughter. It was then that I was reminded of a time that I saw Jillian snooping on my land with an enormous belly.

The Appalachian Arian pack's wind magic is gone because of her. It fades and dwindles by the day.

I sought after the missing child for years. I've called in a lot of debts to get information. The Sanderson realty group owed me dearly, and I called in a favor to Mr. Sanderson. I came up with the offer to buy Loch Bar & Grill, just to hopefully lure her out here, and it worked! The offer wasn't real. Though her bosses don't know that. Mr. Sanderson just believes I want to acquire the building from him once he owns it. The idiot.

So, you see, all is fair in revenge. Now, Jaxon, stand aside.

"No, all isn't fair in revenge. If you want Mira, you will have to go through me," I say, and then I lunge toward Hank.

"I love you," I send in Mira's direction. She's just now getting up from her hard hit, and when she does, I can hear the fog in her mind.

Hank and I snap at one another. We jump around in circles, it seems. Hank's distracting me. He wants to tire me out so he can go for Mira, but that will never happen.

He dies tonight.

***

Mira

I wasn't expecting this to happen. Jaxon said I wasn't a warrior, and I'm starting to realize that means more than me not being able to fight. It means I have no combative skills, either.

Jaxon and Hank are fighting one another, snapping at the other. Their paws are so large, they're equally matched. They're both fighting for something, but I must do something to help. Hank only wants to kill him to get to me. My mother was smart—she knew someone like Hank shouldn't be allowed to live after he killed her mate. She'd tried to end his tirade and, unfortunately, gave life to a new mission in him.

The sky crackles with thunder, lighting it up above us. Rain almost immediately begins to fall on us, and an idea strikes me. Slowly, I'm able to shift back into my human form. No one is paying me any attention, thankfully, and I just need Jaxon to hold him off for a minute. I need him to stick with him if he can.

As the water falls, I lift my hands to the sky. My eyes are on the water, and it slips between my fingertips, over my head. I feel connected to the rain in a way I've never felt before.

As it slips over me, I call to it silently.

I need your help again...

I begin collecting the rain in my hands. The drops stack on top of one another, one by one, weaving a bubble in my hands. As the bubble stretches, my arms widen, and I'm amazed by the sight of the size. It's really working. While I'm forming the bubble, I'm watching Jaxon, and he's losing the fight. He's bleeding from his back legs, and he won't make it much longer.

I'm hurrying, making the bubble as big as I can. When it's as large as I can stand it, I charge Hank. The bubble filled with water rushed over him. Hank is completely caught off guard, and he begins drowning in the water bubble. I'm able to still wield it in my hands, and I'm turning it, around and around. Each time, Hank loses more breath.

Eventually, he succumbs to the water, and I watch the life, what's left of it, fade from his eyes. I release the water, thanking it again for its help, and my arms fall to my side.

Jaxon and I stare at one another, and tears rush to my eyes. He scoops me into his arms, kissing me all over.

"I thought I was going to lose you," he whispers in my ear, and I nibble on the top of his.

"Not today," is all I can say. "I'm sorry for bringing this kind of trouble. You lost some good people today," I mention, looking around at the mayhem brought on by my family.

"And they sacrificed themselves to keep us safe, to keep you safe. Their lives were not taken in vain."

"Sure as hell weren't. Two of them lost their mates a few years back. I have no doubt they're with them now," Pike appears, limping and holding his side, but his positive attitude remains.

Pike claps Jax on the back, and they hold one another up.

"Let's go home," I'm the first to say, and I realize that this is my home. Wherever Jaxon Loch is, is exactly where I want to be.

Epilogue

8 Months Later

"Okay, when Mom gets here, just let her talk, okay? She's kind of a chatty Kathy."

I've done my best to inform Jaxon of how Mom will be when she gets here. She hasn't seen me in eight months, and I know she'll have lots to say. When I told her I was a wolf shifter, she didn't believe me right away. Over the last few months, she's kind of come around to it, but I know the only way for her to believe me is for me to actually show her.

Dad is off on another business trip, as always. I wish I got to spend more time with him, but he's always been a work-a-holic. He's the reason we've had the life we have, so I do my best not to complain.

"I'd be happy to talk to your mother. I'm sure whatever she has to say will be worth hearing." Jax slaps me on my ass and kisses me on the cheek as I finish preparing the cabin's living room for her. She'll stay in our guest bedroom for a few days, although I offered Mama Sue's place, because it was a much easier adjustment than living amongst the wolves, something I was still getting used to.

I quit my job at Sanderson Realty. Beyond not wanting to go back to the city, I couldn't go back and work for a man who was ever in cahoots with Hank. Regardless of the fact, that he didn't know. It left many doors open in my mind about who he really was, and I don't need to return there. I can do real estate from anywhere, and I'm putting together my own company to run out of Sevierville. I know it will be worth it. Plenty of people are trying to buy cabins, or homes, and even have them built. I know a few real estate developers in the area, so I think I'll be set.

Jaxon let me help save the bar and grill, though it wasn't with ease. I was able to pay off the debts the bar had accrued and brought in a marketing team to help get the business circulating in other places outside of the surrounding area. We purchased a mobile food truck, that only served lunch and dinner, to make sure Saturdays and Sundays at our original location maintained its patrons and drew in others who'd sampled the food truck and wanted the restaurant experience. It worked, and the business was starting to profit, and I dare say, thriving.

When I hear a car outside, I know right away it's Mom. I'm nervous but excited to see her since it's been so long. My life has had some major adjustments, but it's also had some quality moments.

"Can you slow your mind? I thought, I was a thinker," I say over my shoulder to Jaxon, whose mind is going crazy, wondering about if my mom will like him, what he should say, and if he should be the first to shift.

"Sorry, I... I just want things to be perfect for her. I know this is important to you."

"You're important to me, so you'll be perfect for her."

Jaxon kisses my lips, and I shudder, hoping we can keep our hands off one another while Mom is here. It seems we're always somewhere naked these days.

Mom closes her door, and I open the door to greet her. She's wearing a pair of jeans and a loose-fitting t-shirt. I've never seen her dressed this way.

"Well, look at you, ready for mountain life," I tease and pull her in for a hug. She squeezes me tight, almost too tight, but she lets go after a few seconds.

"Yes, I am. I had your father buy me these. He's more into casual wear, you know? You must be Jaxon, it's nice to finally meet you," Mom greets Jaxon, and her voice sounds sincere. She's sporting a smile as big as a Cheshire cat, so I know she's happy.

"It's nice to meet you as well. FaceTime videos do nothing for you. You're beautiful," he admires Mom, and she blushes.

"Well, thank you. Now, let's get down to business. I believe there's something you want to show me." Mom gets straight to the point. She'd said the only way she would believe it was if she saw it.

"Coming right up," I agree and take a step onto the porch. My shifts are much quicker. I can almost blink and shift.

I push my arms out to the side, and now my head and body shift at the same time. When I'm completely on the ground, I lay at her feet, and I see tears rush to her eyes. I'm not sure what this means.

"She's beautiful," Mom says, and she gets down to the ground on her knees, rubbing her fingers through my hair.

"Ooh, but her hair is coarse. Should we brush it?" she asks, and Jaxon laughs. I would laugh if I hadn't shifted into my wolf form.

"No, I think she likes to lick it into shape," Jaxon mentions, and he's right, I do.

I shift back onto two legs and grab one of Jaxon's flannel shirts from the living room and close the door behind me.

"I'm sorry I made you miss this part of your life, sweetheart. I know you've forgiven me, but—"

"There are no buts, Mom. Everything happens the way it was supposed to happen. I have my mate, and I have a family who loves me. I truly can't ask for more," I admit with honesty. I've truly never been happier than I am right now.

"Well, I'm glad. Now, tell me more about this mating thing. What exactly is that?"

Jaxon nears me, and wraps his arm around my shoulder, pulling me in for a hug and a kiss. Mom rambles off question after question, like I knew she would. Even with all the changes around me, I'm so happy that some things stayed the same.

"You know you can never get rid of us now, right? Once Mom is used to something, that's it. You've gotta keep us," I whisper to Jaxon as Mom continues her line of questioning. She's not even paying us any attention as she continues her interrogation.

"I told you; we're mated forever and ever. I have the rest of my life with you. I never want to get rid of you. I never want to lose you. Mira, I love you, and your rambling mother is hilarious," Jaxon says. He kisses me on the cheek and then leaves me to take a seat next to Mom.

I have no idea what's to come, but I know I'll face whatever it is with Jaxon by my side. He's the alpha of the Loch pack, but he's my mate and the love of my life...

Thank you for reading **Fated to the Enemy Alpha.**
Did you LOVE this book? Then you will love **Alpha Bound By Fate**!

Discover a bond that defies rules and intensifies with every glance.

Amidst pack conflicts, an Alpha's heart battles for love and duty.

Experience the passion and peril in this gripping tale of love and loyalty.

***You can devour Alpha Bound by Fate for FREE!*
CLICK HERE-https://www.BookHip.com/BTXCMDS**

Here's a sneak peek:

Balancing the duties of an Alpha and the forbidden attraction to my brother's ex, Zoe, isn't easy.

Our fated bond grows stronger each day, complicating my focus on looming threats against my pack.

I'll defend my pack and Zoe at any cost, ready to sacrifice everything for the woman who's become mine.

Get your copy of Alpha Bound by Fate now! https://www.BookHip.com/BTXCMDS

Get a Steamy Alpha Romance for FREE!

I write steamy paranormal romances centered around fated mates... wolves, witches, and any other supernatural being that is in my imagination!

Do you want to be the first to know when I release new books, access to exclusive sneak peeks, and giveaways? Then join my newsletter and get **Alpha Bound by Fate** for Free by signing up!

Get your copy of Alpha Bound by Fate now! https://www.BookHip.com/BTXCMDS

An Enemies to Lovers Steamy Paranormal Romance

Being Alpha is not a simple task and neither is being attracted to your brother's ex.

Even though she's off limits, I struggle to keep my hands off her.

I soon realized we are fated mates with the bond strengthening every day.

My attention should be on finding out who is trying to start a war with my pack.

Now I'm burdened with proving myself to my mate.

Zoe is quiet and reserved at first, but she can't hide her physical reactions.

She drops her guard with me, relaxing and becoming aroused at the same time.

My slightest touch quickens her pulse and her face flushes with desire.

Anyone dumb enough to start a war with me has a death sentence.

I have even more to fight for now than ever.

I will protect what is mine even if I must sacrifice my life for hers

Prologue

Tension filled the hidden convention center that housed The Guild's private meetings. Lazarus, The Guild's head senator, lifted his hands in the atrium to assess the strength of the cloaking spell around the Californian skyscraper.

He could taste the magic in the air; his spell would hold, as it always did, yet he doubted himself, as leaders often did.

Lazarus, as the longest standing Guild leader had had his challenges, and today would be no different. The Guild was created to protect and serve the supernatural and shifter communities. Until the last year or so, Lazarus felt he and his fellow committee members had done that job precisely.

Crime was expected. Too many personalities, too many leaders, and those who want to be in power—of course, there would be... issues. He knew this. He understood this.

But, the rules were clear.

Shifter and supernatural activity should not disrupt human life. It was The Guild's most absolute law for the factions. Human life being disrupted was how wars were started, how genocide was created, and Lazarus had had enough of the bear shifters in the Carolinas.

Time after time, he had been lenient. He'd gone to bat for them when their alpha Hanson decided to separate his pack from the other factions. They went to live in a more secluded part of the mountains because he believed they would thrive and thrive they did.

Unfortunately, Hanson's kindness was taken for weakness, and he was killed in cold blood, found in the middle of the forest, in his bear form. Chills rushed over Lazarus' skin. He, too was a shifter, a tribrid of sorts. Part human, part warlock, and part wolf. Which is how he became the leader of The Guild.

When Hanson met his unfortunate demise a year ago, it caused an uprising in the bear shifter community. He was the only thing keeping the peace between the bear shifters of the Carolinas. Though the line of succession was clear, Hanson's two sons were killed shortly after his death, which left the pack without an alpha.

With no pack leader, the bear shifters became unruly, and lawless in a sense. News of an uprising of crime had gotten back to The Guild, and Lazarus, along with the other leaders of the supernatural factions, must come to an agreement on how to handle them going forward.

The atrium began to fill with shifters. The eagles, phoenixes, wolves, and mountain lion shifters being the most present of the factions. They always came in droves and stood proud as they entered.

Lazarus wasn't familiar with everyone; how could he be? Though, he did have his favorites. Amongst them was his newest and favorite alpha of the Loch pack in the Appalachians, Jaxon. But a heavy cloud surrounded Jaxon. A heaviness Lazarus understood—being a leader had its perks, but it always came at a price.

Following the traffic of the shifters, Lazarus made his way into the meeting room, large enough for 1,000 members, and took his seat in the center of the long wooden panel, surrounded by his peers.

On either side of him were five seats, representing those of the supernatural factions. Witches, wolves, phoenixes, fae, eagles, mountain lions, dragons, gargoyles, hellhounds, and the water folk. When he took his seat, the committee members greeted him with warm and cold greetings, and then he called the meeting to attention by tapping on his microphone.

Shifters and supernaturals scattered around the room, rushing to their seats as the meeting began. The room silenced, the doors of the meeting closed, and Lazarus commenced his opening speech.

"Good morning, shifters and supernaturals. The first and most important thing on our agenda this morning is the bear shifters of the Carolinas. Their activity over the last year has been monitored, and our findings have conveyed high crime rates, excessive thefts, and--"

"Murder, lots and lots of murder..." a sinister male voice roared as it entered the room. Gasps of shock and awe erupted throughout the room as the voice revealed itself.

"You do not belong here!" Lazarus rose from his seat, his skin prickling as though a shift was imminent.

To his right, Phaedra, a fellow witch, latched onto his arm. She'd seen him lose his cool one too many times, and hoped for everyone in this room's sake that he did not in this moment.

Lazarus allowed Phaedra's touch to soothe him, as only she could, because their relationship ran much deeper than that of leader and committee member, and his temperament instantly softened.

"You're right—we don't belong here, and that's exactly why we're here." boasted Cedric, one of the bear shifters. Asserting his stance as he and several of his pack members, who had completely shifted, strutted down the center aisle of the meeting room.

Lazarus was thankful that humans within a 30-mile radius wouldn't be able to see anyone who was in their shift, nor would they see the convention center. What they would see was an old and run down building, that looked too dangerous to enter.

With the bear shifters coming to the meeting they weren't invited to, there were two things he needed to address as soon as possible.

Someone had leaked the meeting to one of the bear shifters.

And, their security around the building and inside wasn't as tight as he'd believed it to be.

"Cedric, since you're here, pray tell... who told you about this secret meeting?" Lazarus' question hung in the air, curiosity evident in his tone.

Cedric continued his way down the aisle, his teeth clenched as tightly as his fists that were balled at his side.

"That's neither here nor there, old man. Heed my words; until the bear shifters are offered a spot on your pretentious little counsel, we'll continue to wreak havoc. We're disregarded, and disrespected, all because we prefer to live in our shifted forms, rather than our human forms."

"No, be clear; you're disregarded because of your lack of care for human life. You, even if it is a small part, are human, yet you do nothing to care for them, to protect them. You have your own agenda, and you use it to destroy instead of helping to maintain the balance," Phaedra interrupted. Even she'd heard enough.

"Oh, the little lap dog speaks for her master now, does she Lazarus?" Cedric teased, his thick and dark eyebrows forming into a menacing scowl.

"You wouldn't say that to someone with real claws, would you, Cedric?"

Fjord, leader of the gargoyles, jumped atop the table, his claws outstretched.

"Please, Fjord, you're too righteous to take a swipe at me. You heard what I said...give us a seat or--"

"We don't negotiate with criminals or shifter terrorists. You'll be given a seat on the board when you show more regard for human life, even your own human lives. Until then, there's nothing to discuss. Now leave, before your punishment becomes something far worse than meeting banishment!" Lazarus' voice carried over the crowd, his chest heaving up and down as he awaited Cedric's response.

"I love a little rift, don't you boys?" Cedric teasingly asked his pack, over his shoulder. His hungry bear brethren chomping at the bit to cause violence in a sacred place.

"Anyone who follows Cedric into mischief and mayhem will also reap the consequences. He's no alpha, and even he answers to someone," Lazarus said the words everyone else already knew to be true. Cedric wasn't a leader—no. He was following the orders of someone else; that much was very clear.

Though he'd always been a bit of a wild card, Cedric hadn't become "the front man" until after Hanson and his two sons were killed. He was an unguided youth, and an even more lost adult now. There had to be someone guiding his choices... all the wrong choices.

"I may not be an alpha, but I speak for the pack now. Get 'em!" Cedric commanded, and he and his bear brothers rushed forward, toward The Guild with all their might, sealing the fate of the Carolina bear shifters...

CLICK HERE to get Alpha Bound by Fate
https://www.BookHip.com/BTXCMDS

Printed in Great Britain
by Amazon